GW00976005

SPINE –
CHILLERS

NORFOLK

Edited by Rob Harding

First published in Great Britain in 2016 by:

 Young**Writers**

Remus House
Coltsfoot Drive
Peterborough
PE2 9BF
Telephone: 01733 890066
Website: www.youngwriters.co.uk
All Rights Reserved
Book Design by Ashley Janson
© Copyright Contributors 2016
SB ISBN 978-1-78624-125-2

Printed and bound in the UK by BookPrintingUK
Website: www.bookprintinguk.com

FOREWORD

Enter, Reader, if you dare...

For as long as there have been stories there have been
ghost stories. Writers have been trying scare their readers
for centuries using just the power of their imagination.
For Young Writers' latest competition Spine-Chillers
we asked students to come up with their own spooky
tales, but with the tricky twist of using just 100 words!

They rose to the challenge magnificently and this resulting
collection of haunting tales will certainly give you the
creeps! From friendly ghosts and Halloween adventures
to the gruesome and macabre, the young writers in this
anthology showcase their creative writing talents.

Here at Young Writers our aim is to encourage creativity
and to inspire a love of the written word, so it's great to
get such an amazing response, with some absolutely
fantastic stories. We will now choose the top 5 authors
across the competition, who will each win a Kindle Fire.

I'd like to congratulate all the young authors in *Spine-
Chillers - Norfolk* - I hope this inspires them to continue
with their creative writing. And who knows, maybe
we'll be seeing their names alongside Stephen
King on the best seller lists in the future...

Jenni Bannister

Editorial Manager

CONTENTS

DISS HIGH SCHOOL, DISS

FAKENHAM ACADEMY, FAKENHAM

FRAMINGHAM EARL HIGH SCHOOL, NORWICH

HELLESDON HIGH SCHOOL, NORWICH

KING EDWARD VII ACADEMY, KING'S LYNN

LITCHAM SCHOOL, KING'S LYNN

LONG STRATTON HIGH SCHOOL, NORWICH

SPRINGWOOD HIGH SCHOOL, KING'S LYNN

THE MINI SAGAS

THE THING

It was right behind me! Or was it next to me? You couldn't tell in this dark gloomy forest but all I knew was that there was something extremely evil bounding right up to me, ready to kill! I now realised that it must've been herding me into the darker parts of the evil forest. As I was running the darkness was closing all around me. I realised I had a painful stitch right on the side of my ribcage but I kept on running for my life! I heard a deep growl, it was there!

BEN GAUNT (12)
Diss High School, Diss

ESCAPE

'We've been interrupted with an important news broadcast. There has been an escape from an asylum. A mentally ill man...'
'Honey come look at this,' I said.
'Wow, doesn't look like a good night to be walking around.' He was interrupted by a rumble of thunder and a blood-curdling scream.
'Someone help me, it's him; the murderous, mentally ill man!' Another spine-tingling scream arose from the poor woman, as the crazy man devoured his latest victim.
With the woman's arm in his hand, he turned and said, 'You're next.'
The murderer's maniacal laugh made my arm tingle.

BETH DENNIS
Diss High School, Diss

Avery

Avery's torch cut through the darkness like a knife. It illuminated thick, sticky pools of scarlet carelessly splat on the walls and floors. The air was foul with death and iron; it made Avery gag. Gruesome mauled bodies lay lifeless on the ground. Then she saw it: a repulsive creature from deep within the Underworld. Its eyes were black holes on its pale, skeletal face. It started to crawl towards her, whispering words of poison. Blood spurted horrifically from its mouth. Fear stiffened Avery's body as the creature spat disgustingly at her. And then... a scream. And darkness.

JOHANNA DAWN BARNETT
Diss High School, Diss

Sudden Death

Many years ago, on a cold winter's day, it was dark, gloomy and miserable. Walking through the churchyard I heard noises. I looked around, no one. Feeling mystified, I went to the dungeon where I heard ear-piercing noises. *Ding-dong!* Within the blink of an eyelid something grabbed my leg. I continued to go down the old, spiral staircase. Waiting around the corner was the fright of my life. I screamed, it echoed up the stairs. I lay on my back, shaking. They enclosed me, I could feel their breath on my face. My life had come to this.

ELLIE LEEPER (12)
Diss High School, Diss

THE LOST DEAD GIRL FIXATED TO ONE GOLDEN CHEST

Years ago a girl named Ivy committed murder, late Friday night. A brave soldier scared her away to a faraway tunnel, never to be seen again. My heart started beating, like my heart was shouting at me. I realised I was in a tunnel, a long winding tunnel. Suddenly, I noticed a shadow along the wall. It darted off quickly, like it could sense me looking at it. 'Argh!' I heard a scream. I ran forward to see a chest before me.

It then boomed out, 'Only mortals shall pass.' My body turned red. They didn't realise I was dead.

ELEANOR BUDDS (13)
Diss High School, Diss

THE TOWN OF NO RETURN

I stole stealthily like a cat in the night, through abandoned streets as twilight invaded quiet corners. Congealed blood covered walls. Contorted bodies lay on the street. A torrent of questions ran through my fevered mind. Corrupting smells penetrated my nostrils. Dusk fell. I resolved to enter the building stranded in silence. Satanic shadows malevolently lurked, swarming like insects, preying on my consciousness. My mind slipped into lunacy. Blinding flashes of light paralysed me but I managed to flee. I felt flooded with relief. Then I realised there was no escape. The town was a trap. I awaited my fate!

ETHAN EVERSON-GERMANY
Diss High School, Diss

TRAPPED

The pain is growing stronger. My heart thumping, thumping, thumping. My head hurts. What's happening to me? I try to get up. I can't. Help! The room around me is spinning. My once blue eyes are shallow. For a second I hear footsteps. And then a bang. Was that a gun? There's no escaping now. The thoughts of my family run through my mind. I imagine their happy faces the day I said 'I do'. I'm never going to see them again. A tear trickles down my porcelain skin. The bang becomes a person. The black silhouette peers down above me.

GEORGIA CLARK (16)
Diss High School, Diss

THE CHILL

I trudged along the gravel to the ancient church when I heard a blood-curdling scream. It broke the silence immediately. I froze, almost paralysed; I couldn't let fear overcome me. I began to sprint, my breath increased as I approached the church. I tugged open the door and ran inside, for all I knew something could be lurking behind me. I needed to call Charlie and tell him I had arrived when a shiver ran down my spine. I could feel the warm breath creeping around my neck. I turned but only to see nothing, the door slammed shut.

DAISY NIXON
Diss High School, Diss

UNTITLED

I woke up to the sound of silence. Darkness was everywhere. All of a sudden the noise of my alarm clock filled my room. *I didn't set that,* I thought. As I reached out to turn it off, I felt a cold ghostly hand already there. Terrified, I lent over to switch on the light but nothing happened. Shaking with fear I crawled under my duvet wishing this nightmare would end. Suddenly a horrifying thought entered my mind that this was only just the beginning of a horror story...

MOLLY NIXON (13)
Diss High School, Diss

ALONE

I was walking through the woods, alone. Leaves rustling as I walked. My torch flickered as the batteries began to run out. I picked up the pace, but soon stopped. The rustling continued; fear overwhelmed me. I was alone I began once again after assuring myself it was a cat but I stopped suddenly just to check. The rustling continued after I stopped. I began to run as fast as I could, but I tripped over. Falling to the ground I saw a shadow standing over me, I looked up to see what it was, I screamed.

PHOEBE JOANNE TYLDESLEY (15)
Diss High School, Diss

An Encounter In The Night

It was about midnight as I began to return home. The sky was black, no moon visible. A light drizzle started to fall. In the distance dog barks echoed and a wailing siren rang out. I continued down the path towards the single flickering lamp, which bathed the path in rippling light, casting strange shadows. Behind me, something watching. I whirled around. Nothing. I turned back to continue home, but a strange cowled figure blocked my path, holding a knife. I ran, rapidly in the opposite direction but slipped on the newly dampened surface. Menacingly the figure moved over me...

JOSEPH KEELEY (14)
Diss High School, Diss

The Old Asylum

The asylum was really strange. It was old and surprisingly cool. Then there was a noise, it made me jump out of my skin. Whatever it was, it was getting closer. The air became thin and my breathing increased as I tried to contain myself against screaming and running out the door. The next thing I knew I had a sharpened piece of metal and a torch shining into the darkness. The door slammed open but nothing was there! I sat, scared, and then I felt something inhuman grab my feet from under the ward bed. My breathing suddenly stopped.

CALLUM NUNN
Diss High School, Diss

ALONE

You know when you're alone. He said he'd come back. But here I was, alone. The fading light left me in a pitch-black forest. I stood facing the way he had left. I could hear my heart beat in the silence, but that was it. It was a short, bright light that caught my attention, the light shone on a dark, mysterious figure straight ahead of me. My life flashed before me as if my life was to end. I knew behind me was the last person I'd ever see. I screamed but not a whisper was let out.

ISOBEL ROSE LINTON (12)
Diss High School, Diss

THE FOG MAN

I tread through the dense marshland, searching blindly for my rucksack. *Rustle!* I turn round, but I can't see anything. The eerie mist engulfs me with fear. I stay rooted to the spot, paralysed, as if I'm being controlled. I'm shivering so violently I can hardly walk. *Rustle!* Alert, I turn round to be greeted by a man with oddly distorted clothes on. 'Hello?' I whisper. I try to sound brave but my teeth are chattering so hard all that comes out is a squeaky voice.
'Goodbye,' rasps the man.
'No!' That was my last word. The mystery travels on.

MILES HOLLIDAY (11)
Diss High School, Diss

THE DEEP CAVE

Drip! goes the water as I'm walking through the darkness of the cave. Endless rows of darkness lay before me. I wonder to myself, *is there an end to this horror?* A shiver goes down my spine. There in the darkness I see a glowing light. 'Who's there?'
A ghostly voice replies, 'I would run child.' I turn around, facing the slanted slope. I climb down and run straight at it, as fast as I can, not daring to look behind me. I climb the slope.
The ghost bellows, 'I will get you, boy.' I run. Is this the end?

CAMERON BROWN (11)
Diss High School, Diss

LOST

Owls hooted mysteriously, cocking their heads and listening to the sound of deadly silence. My boots were caked in mud; they sucked against the earth underfoot and skidded whilst I tried to get footing. The dusty roots of the trees were reaching out to grab my feet and pull me towards them; their branches and strands of coiled ivy stretched out to strangle me. I shrank back, wrapping my arms around myself. I felt a cold breath go down my collar, my spine tingled and hairs prickled on my neck. A pair of amber eyes stared at me...

AMY ADSHEAD (11)
Diss High School, Diss

DWARF FRIGHT

One black, stormy night I woke up from a crash of lightning. My parents were having a night walk, I was all alone with my kitten. I started doing my homework as I had nothing better to do. My kitten miaowed for food, so I gave her some.

A few hours had passed and I started to worry about my mum and dad. Suddenly, the power went out, and my house fell into complete darkness. I looked out of my bedroom window and saw two red, scary dwarfs in the misty fog. They were walking towards my house…

Oh no!

ANNA WICKS (11)
Diss High School, Diss

ON THE EDGE

We were stood on the edge and we looked around, with no other option: we had to jump! Darkness was slowly swallowing the sun and the sky was heavy with clouds. Three hours before, in tragic naivety, our friend was captured. We didn't know the reason behind it but we knew we were now involved. As a swarm of men gathered around us but we managed to dive underneath a grasping hand. Our feet pounded the ground as we fled the scene, although eventually we reached a ledge. The next decision was fatal. We knew what we had to do!

EMILY REAVELL (16)
Diss High School, Diss

THE DOOR

I stand, frozen, shaking, battered and cracked. The bony wooden door bares its teeth at me. It's old and withered but it's all that stands between me and whatever's in there. A deadly red glow glares through the cracks. I need to go. I need to go, but my feet aren't moving; the thing behind the door is moving. The muffled, rabid moans of a hungry madman. I can hear it dragging itself across the floor. Getting nearer. It knows I'm here. The noise stops. My heart is a drum, beating in the sickening silence. The handle begins to turn...

EDWARD DARRALL (14)
Diss High School, Diss

THE BARN

Trudging through the November mud, Natward saw a barn. *I can wait out the rain in there,* he thought. He lifted the rusty iron latch and pushed the solid oak door open. As he entered, the smell of damp straw and animal dung hit him. Suddenly, something rushed into the dark behind a bale of hay. Natward saw a hay fork leaning against the wall. He grabbed it tight and pointed it towards the bale. 'Hello,' he asked, 'is anyone there?'
As he was beginning to let down his guard a voice replied, 'No, Seamus is not here.'

ROBERT BALDING (15)
Diss High School, Diss

THE FOREST

It was midnight, I was walking through the gloomy woods and heard the distinctive ring of church bells through the mist. I suddenly heard a leaf crunch near me. 'Hello?' I called. Silence. My heart started racing. I sprinted towards the church, leaves crunching behind me. They were getting closer and closer. Soon I had no energy. The crunching of leaves had stopped. My phone began to vibrate in my pocket as I reached the church. 'I'll be home soon Mum, I promise.' The phone screen went dim. That's when it all went dark.

DANIEL DEBENHAM (14)
Diss High School, Diss

LIGHTS OUT

The jolt of the floor woke me. As I tried to sit up I realised I was inside of somewhere that wasn't designed for movement. Above me I could faintly hear voices, crying voices. The wailing was interrupted by a dull thud above me, much like sand crashing onto a board. Bewilderment gave way to panic as it dawned on me that wherever I was, I was trapped. Voices became muffled as thuds were more frequent, it grew apparent that my shrill screams were inaudible. Before long the only sound filling my ears was my thumping heartbeat.

LAUREN DENNIS (14)
Diss High School, Diss

WOLVES...

One night in the middle of winter, at exactly 2:56am, I was warily trudging up a hill in a forest, the moon dead ahead. Trees whistled in the wind, wolves howled in the distance. I felt like I had eyes concentrated on me. Suddenly, I saw the shape of a wolf appear in front of the moon; it ran. Within a second it appeared at the top of the hill. It stopped. It howled, it saw me, then ran again in my direction! I turned and ran. Wolves appeared in front, to my left and to my right...

CHARLIE BOWEN (15)
Diss High School, Diss

THE TICKING OF THE CLOCK

In summer, the sun rises at six o'clock in the morning. Every morning. But today, today the sun decided to have a day off. Cower behind the horizon's sanctuary, weep. In the unbroken light of blackness, fears are no longer imagination. Your mind wriggles and fights and rages to create a world in which to live... or die? Frustration, pent up and contained broken free. Madness. The incessant ticking of the clocks. *Tick. Tick. Tick.* The stamping of the feet. The shrieking of the insane. The biting of the nails. In the darkness, some are afraid. I am ecstatic.

WILLIAM JOHNSON (14)
Diss High School, Diss

MYSTERY GRAVEYARD

One misty, foggy night I was walking with my mate towards a graveyard. It was where my dad died two years ago. I could not see anything, I turned around and my friend was gone! I called his name but no one came. Suddenly, I heard this noise, a strange noise and there was a cold breeze on my neck. I turned around and there was my dead dad's ghost. He had a knife in his hand. 'Arrr!' He ripped my guts out!

HARVEY WHYMARK (12)
Diss High School, Diss

FEARS

Everyone has fears: death, spiders. They were my fears. One day they surrounded me. Every night I would lay in bed looking around. There was always one spider sitting there, looking at me like I was evil. One night a storm came! *Boom! Thud!* That was all I heard. I looked up at the spider, but there wasn't just him. There were thousands of them; red-eyed, staring into my soul. I pulled the covers over my head and fell asleep. I woke up bitten all over. It happened again the next night, except I never woke up!

MARY RICE (13)
Diss High School, Diss

GONE STARGAZING

It had been an idyllic day. Billy and Dan had been walking in the pleasant, summery fields. They pitched their tent on a golden mound and gazed at the stunning pink sunset. The campfire blazed high and jolly into the dusk. After that, silence. No more crickets chirped. The clouds loomed, unwelcoming and imperious. Since stargazing was impossible, the pair peered into their binoculars at the distant town's glow. 'What was that?' cried Billy. A dark shape blocked out the light and grew. The boys huddled up in their tents as the events that would change their entire life unfolded horribly.

BOBBY GREATHEAD (12)
Diss High School, Diss

HUNTED

I ran, I just ran, the more I did the more he closed in. I had no idea at first, but soon it was a nightmare come true. He was throwing metal knives, it looked like he had an endless supply of them. He did. His name was Kraven The Hunter. He said he was sent to kill me but it felt personal. I am a bank manager from New York. I ran into my home made of compressed obsidian. I collected my supplies: food, water and my kitana. I ran out, only to be impaled by him.

WILLIAM KENNETH TATE (13)
Diss High School, Diss

THE STALKING SHADOW

It was getting darker in the forest, so I decided to walk back home. Suddenly, I heard a twig crunch beside me. I called out but no one answered. I carried on, but now there was something beside me, constantly following me. Every time I turned around there was no one there. Now, two years on, it is still stalking me, hiding in the shadows, waiting for the chance to pounce, unexpectedly.

EVAN VOYCE (12)
Diss High School, Diss

WILL BE MISSED

Lullaby Lodge, second of December, four hours left. It's dark, snowy.
'Where's Jack?' Samantha replies, 'Must be sick, I'm guessing!'
'Do you think he's...?' I wish Axel didn't say that.
Before he can finish, I shout 'Stop!' at the top of my lungs.
The group and I decide to head up to the lodge on Lullaby Hill. You might be able to tell that this place gives us all the creeps. Two of the seven are gone, two hours left. 'Where are they?'
Everyone's scared. 'John! Jacob?'
I was knocked out but I eventually wake up. 'Jack, is that you?'

JOE CATES (11)
Diss High School, Diss

INTO THE LAKE

As Lucy shivered, the icy winter wind howled and the crunching of leaves filled the dark and weary forest. Lucy stumbled on a fallen branch and rolled into the frost-covered lake. The shattering of ice echoed across the trees. Ghostly figures drifted into Lucy's mind, she screamed but then she realised maybe only the creatures dragging her under would be able to hear.

When Lucy awoke, she guessed it must have been a dream. She stood up to get breakfast. As she looked into the mirror, she found the water was no longer water, it was blood!

EVIE ROSE HENSSER (11)
Diss High School, Diss

LATE HOME

It was getting dark. Jack was already late home so he decided to take a short cut through the eerie graveyard. He stepped around crumbling tombs and gravestones, until he reached a building. The door was wide open. Jack stepped inside, he put his hand on the cold damp wall; since there was no light he felt his way around. Then he heard a *bang!* He turned around. The door had closed. He went over to try and open it. It was locked, he was trapped! Then he felt a drop on his head. It wasn't water though, it was blood!

HENRY FREDERICK HURST (11)
Diss High School, Diss

Ghost Revenge

Hi, I'm Jake. I'm twelve years old. I was trick or treating with my friends but I was soon starting to regret it. My friends dared me to knock on this cottage door and I was dragged inside by a man about thirty years old. He wouldn't let me go! My last words were a piercing scream and the sight of an axe on my throat. I'm now dead. Ghastly, you might say. But I'm going back for revenge. I'm going to haunt him. He is in for it now! His name is Mike. Goodnight Mike, sleep tight. Ha! Ha! Ha!

Zoe Cruickshank (13)
Diss High School, Diss

Alone

Have you ever been all alone? Standing there, alone. You look up to see a distant face, you comprehend it's calling you. A breath leaves the mouth of the well-known stranger. A circle of condensation appears. You gaze at it bleakly. A sudden rush of wind wraps around you as if you're a present to be opened at Christmas. Suddenly, a hand grasps you. Fear rushes through your cold-blooded veins. You're gone! Even when you think you're alone you're not. You are never alone.

Georgia Mackelden (14)
Diss High School, Diss

DARK ALLEYS

One night there was a boy walking down an alleyway, he heard something coming from smoke and then there was an 'Arghhh!' The next day there was a crime scene. The police were eating their lunch and a girl came along and went in there. She went into the crime scene and saw a dead boy, she saw smoke as well so she went into the smoke and a cold hand touched her. She couldn't see him but he said, 'Don't scream.' A few seconds later there was a girl's scream, she was dead, her head had been chopped off.

JACK GLANVILLE (11)
Diss High School, Diss

AMY'S STORY

One night there was a girl called Amy. She was eleven years old and was playing in the frost. There was a man staring at Amy. She said, 'Why are you staring at me?'
Suddenly, her mum called her. 'Time you came in.'
Amy went in and said, 'Where are you going?'
'I am going to the shop.'
'OK.'
When her mum was gone the man said, 'You are coming with me.'
When her mum came back, Amy was gone.
It was three days later. Amy said, 'Where are we?' The man just punched her.

YAZMIN BALDOCK (11)
Diss High School, Diss

Always With You

I'm always with you, staring at you with large cloudy eyes. You saw me once, in the dead of night, hunching over you with a hole in my stomach, revealing shattered bones and rotting organs. My jagged teeth formed a hellish grin. You tried to scream, but I covered your mouth with my claws. You thought you'd never forget the sight of me. You'll see me again, in the darkness, whispering to you. My words crawl into your mind, controlling you like a puppet. I'll guide you to insanity, for all eternity never escaping. I'm always with you.

GRACE FALLOWS (13)
Diss High School, Diss

The Ghostly Fog

This morning my friend dared me to go into the forest at night. I did it, I sat in the forest before it happened. A mysterious fog circled me and it was quickly getting closer! I did the only thing I could think of, I ran through the fog, it burned. There were birds flapping madly. Suddenly, I ran headlong into a tree. I could taste blood, smell it, feel it as it trickled down my legs. I could smell blood, sweat and burning. A hand grabbed me by the neck. It was my friend, Alannah, also covered in blood...

MEGAN PARKER (11)
Diss High School, Diss

GHOST IN THE AIR

One misty day in Witchfield, there was a boy called Raheem who went to an abandoned mansion. It had shattered windows, creaky floors and an old, creepy painting. He went inside the creepy room and there were filthy beds, dirty walls and stained glass windows. Then, a few minutes later, he saw a shadow in a distance and investigated. He was then worried and scared by an evil spirited ghost! He tried to get out of the abandoned mansion but he couldn't because the ghost locked all the doors... He was doomed!

NIYAZ MIAH (11)
Diss High School, Diss

THE TUNNEL

It was pitch-black, I couldn't see anything. My whole body was ice-cold with fright. I started to stumble around the very small and very narrow tunnel. Every time I touched the walls they crumbled at my fingertips. All I could hear was the sound of water dripping from the roof of the tunnel. I felt an icy breath on my neck. My hairs stood on end. There was no wind anywhere. What could it be? Slowly I turned around. A cold hand touched my shoulder. A low voice whispered, 'It is time for you to join us!'

ISABELLA LITEWSKA (11)
Diss High School, Diss

THE MANSION

'What was that?' said Derek.
'What was what?' said Connor.
'Don't tell me you didn't hear that. Just follow me.'
They ran into a fence. Behind the fence was a mansion. 'Let's investigate this,' said Derek. They climbed over the back fence. As soon as this happened, Derek heard whispers and the sky went pitch-black, like the stars had disappeared. Suddenly, Derek heard a scream and saw a tall, black figure looking out the window. Suddenly, a window smashed. Derek went towards it, there was a stone and on the stone it said: 'You're next!'

JAKUB CHROSTOWSKI (13)
Diss High School, Diss

GRAVEYARD

As I walk through the forest I come to a graveyard. I hear footsteps behind. Hoping it's a dream I turn around but the shriek of my own scream pierces through my ears. The floor of the graveyard trembles as I fall to the floor. *Is this real life?* I think to myself. All of a sudden it goes quiet, the footsteps stop. I am still lying on the cold, wet concrete of a gravestone. I feel a thump coming from the grave. *Bang!* The ground comes up from behind me. What is it?

LEAH FOX (11)
Diss High School, Diss

THE NIGHT IT ALL HAPPENED

As I sit by an old rotten tree all I can hear is my heart beating from all the shock. As I get up I bump into a gravestone. I start to walk out of the churchyard but it feels like someone is following me. I didn't turn around just in case but I now wish I had as all I can hear is someone breathing on me. Then suddenly, a cold, wet hand is on my shoulder. Before I know it there is blood dripping down my clothes. Then it gets me...

CHLOE SOMERVILLE-HEMSLEY
Diss High School, Diss

A SCHOOL BUS OF NIGHTMARES

It's a misty, dark day. I hear gunshots so I go to see where they are coming from. Earlier I heard a school bus go by. Are the shots at the bus? Two minutes later I find a child's body and a bus. With fading sirens in the distance I hide behind a massive boulder, looking at the questionable school bus. I look over, the driver is forced out of the bus then he gets shot. I think all the children are dead, then the next thing I know is...

FRASER WATSON (11)
Diss High School, Diss

I'm Just A Boy

The hand, all he could feel. It gouged at his flesh as he screamed. He felt empty, like it was draining all of his happy thoughts. His mum's laugh, his dog's whining, his last smile. It released, he fell. Something grey crept up his arm, it hardened as he tried to move. A voice filled his mind, his mum's. 'You useless child, this is what I should have done to you from the day you were born.'
He screamed. Nothing. No one could help him now, this was his doom.

MAE CLARK (11)
Diss High School, Diss

Dolly Trouble

It's moving day! I can't wait! But little do I know that it isn't going to be the day I'm expecting...
I'd seen the house already and it's epic, but I soon see something that gives me the creeps, a doll! It's holding a knife. I run to the kitchen screaming. When I open the fridge... the doll! It's there in the fridge, I shout for help, but no one answers. I explore the house and nothing is there. Just then a gust of wind shuts the door and I can see blood dripping... 'Mum!'

PARIS WOOLTERTON (11)
Diss High School, Diss

CHAMBER OF HORROR

Screech! It's coming from the door. *Bang!* I've been locked in the Chamber of Horror. I hear talking. Is someone else in here with me? I see no one apart from the wax works. They're reaching out, trying to grab me. I run for my life. What am I going to do? A cold breeze is making its way down my spine, a hand tiptoes up my shoulder and grabs me. I don't move one bit. I make no noise. The hand is dripping with blood, its veins are sticking out; the bony hand squeezes me and turns me around. 'Argh!'

ANYA MOLDEN (12)
Diss High School, Diss

THE DARES AWAKE

It was a dark, foggy night, nothing to be seen but woods. These three children, around the age of thirteen, dared each other to go into the spine-chilling woods where, according to myth, there's an abandoned mansion where people say a tall horrifying man lives. He is gruesome and brutal, he wears a hockey mask with a suit. The three kids went looking for his mansion but it was nowhere to be seen. So, one of the kids said, 'Let's play hide-and-seek.' As soon as they played it, one of them went missing. There were screams everywhere.

BRANDON HUNT
Diss High School, Diss

A Figure In The Dark

It was a misty November night. I sat in front of the burning campfire, eating fluffy marshmallows, my favourite! The forest air brought a chill up my back. I waited in silence for Sam to come out her tent. What happened still gives me dreadful nightmares. A blood-curdling scream came from the tent. I ran to find out what was happening but I still was not sure what was going on. A nasty aroma burst through my nose. There was Sam, pale as snow. Dead! Out of the gloom I saw a figure coming. I knew I had to run.

ELIZABETH ARMSTRONG (12)
Diss High School, Diss

The Being

Its jet-black feathers clung to its back. I saw it watching me, its beady eyes clung to me like wet clothes. It squawked and flew off. *To where?* I thought. A bang sounded. A hoof clattered on the cobble. He stepped out into the open. Red-skinned and sporting great black horns and a devilish smile. Fangs protruded from his blood-splattered mouth, an upside-down cross hung from his stumpy neck, his eyes on fire with rage. A pentagram was tattooed on his forehead. Its crooked hands had wretched claws. He advanced upon me.

BENJAMIN KENNEDY (14)
Diss High School, Diss

-18°C

The icy chill slaps me as I yank open the perpetually sticky freezer door. This is easily the worst part of my job. I scurry into the frozen store room, bitterly regretting leaving my coat in the hall. The hairs on my arms stand to attention as I venture deeper in; only when I'm ready to leave do I realise that the cold is not their sergeant. Time slows down. I turn, with mounting trepidation, just in time to catch a glimpse of the faceless shadow by the door. I see the door lock before I hear the bang.

CHANTELLE LEE (17)
Diss High School, Diss

SILENT NIGHT FEARSOME FRIGHT

Ever sensed another despite being desperately alone? 11:59. Locked from the haven of glowing lights, this insignificant shortcut seems a very significant hell, with no December festivities. The shop's icy milk spreads chills through my body. The whisper of an eerie noise. Was that my footstep? I fumble for my phone. Gone. Biting beads dribble through my fingers; streaming like a tap. A branch snaps. I walk faster, my breath harsh, visible. Deafening silence. Devoid of security. Haunted by trepidation. Suddenly I perceive milk splattering on the cobblestones, where only darkness shines. A gruesome hand rests on my shoulder...

LILY HARRIS (14)
Diss High School, Diss

HIDE-AND-SEEK

'Ready or not, here I come!' I screeched into the thick fog of the forest. The cool breeze tickled my arms as I rushed between towering trees, in search of hidden friends. 'Hello?' I called into the darkness. The air, once thick with joyful giggles, was now replaced with piercing silence. From the silence emerged a growing sound of footsteps following me; the echo growing louder and louder, closer and closer. The darkness swallowed my path as I became painfully aware that I was lost and alone, except for the footsteps directly behind me now, I turned...

LIBBY HAMLING (16)
Diss High School, Diss

WHAT ON EARTH (OR MARS, FOR THAT MATTER!)?

As the unsuspecting boy walks into school, something is amiss. Yves is extraordinary short, has red tinted eyes, the worst Russian accent ever and he drinks through his index finger. Mikel befriends him, although he's different. Mikel suspects Yves isn't who he seems to be. When Yves realises Mikel's suspicions a fight breaks out. Fists fly, legs flail and at that moment, there's a thunderstorm. A strange silhouette is illuminated by a flash of lightning. Perhaps? It couldn't be, could it? Surely not? Is it really?
Even today, I'm still not sure what happened to me when the aliens came.

LORNA BAKER (12)
Diss High School, Diss

Night At The Hospital

I came out the hospital, the guy who stabbed me ran past. There were zombies groaning, dripping blood, chasing the criminal. I hid in the reception and came back out five minutes later. All that was left was his head. Again I went back inside and sat down with a sigh of relief. Suddenly, the scream of a zombie about to kick me made me drop to the floor. He grabbed me and bit my arm off. I screamed, then I felt nothing but pain. I slowly approached the receptionist. Then, *bang* went the shotgun but I was still standing unharmed.

JAMES GOODERHAM (15)
Diss High School, Diss

The Man I Saw In My Dream

A room with no escaping light and none entering. Is this the place he spoke of, the man in my dream? Suddenly, light. A blinding, pure white light. But still nothing devoid of life. Still blinded by the light, I try to feel my way around. I'm tied up! My hands above my head, feet shackled together. You get taught what to do in these situations but when it's actually happening, how can you think rationally? 'Hello?' It falls into my lap, part of it anyway. I look up and there's the rest. The man I saw in my dream...

MADDISON PAICE MCQUE (14)
Diss High School, Diss

Girl Missing

Only last week I'd seen the words 'Girl Missing' plastered over newspapers. One evening I was walking home when a cloak of fog and darkness enveloped me without warning. I quickened my pace and decided to take a shortcut through the forest. I'd been walking for roughly five minutes when I tripped over an object on the frozen ground. Gingerly, I looked to see what I'd stumbled upon. Then I saw her. I saw a cold, bloodstained, stiff, dead body; Girl Missing's body. I let out a loud, blood-curdling scream and ran from the scene, terrified.

Lucy Pawsey (14)
Diss High School, Diss

Charlie Was Murdered On Thursday!

In 2015 a boy called Charlie lived in Diss, he was twelve years old. Charlie saw a dark shadow but didn't turn around. Suddenly, a murderer came and grabbed Charlie's shoulder. Next, the murderer grabbed Charlie's mouth for thirty seconds until Charlie couldn't breathe.
Charlie's mum came upstairs and called Charlie for dinner so the murderer hid in Charlie's cupboard. Charlie couldn't breathe, Charlie's mum went to his room and his mum saw Charlie was pale. His mum got her phone and called A&E but Charlie died.

Louise Conquest (11)
Diss High School, Diss

On Your Own

'Breaking news: A serial killer has just escaped from prison. If you see him call 999 straight away. This is what he looks like...'
'I don't feel safe any more. I'll go get some fresh air,' then I see a dark figure standing outside the window in the snow. He fits the description of the murderer. I pick up the phone immediately. He is moving closer until just his footprints are outside. I see the murderer's reflection...

William Beale (12)
Diss High School, Diss

Home

Your home, where you repose in blissful ignorance. Yet, have you ever been alone; abandoned in that home with nothing but deafening silence surrounding the relentless heartbeat of the clock? Inexplicably, the ignorance mutates into a gut-wrenching shudder with the realisation that 'home' is not so safe. Your breath quickens. You feel an icy chill as shadows crawl up your spine, lengthening your back into a posture of alert vulnerability. You descend into a frenzy of terror; your eyes searching the darkness, while some benighted voice manipulates you to ignore the fear. Except, you've never asked... whose voice?

Emma Carpenter (14)
Diss High School, Diss

THE BARN

The air in the barn was thick and stale. Strips of crimson paint lay on the floor, exposing the rotting wood of the walls. A dark fog swept around my feet, stopping me from moving. Something wanted me to stay in that room. A large shadow appeared on the end wall. I heard footsteps but couldn't find their owner. Foul breath hit my cheek, sending a shiver down my neck. 'I've finally got you.'

ROWAN LILI WHITTINGTON (14)
Diss High School, Diss

THE IMPENETRABLE
DARKNESS OF DEATH

I jerked awake, aware that I wasn't where I should be. I was on immediate alert, the taste of blood filled my mouth and an odd feeling surged down my spine. I was immediately aware of the smell of damp in the room and that I was tied up unable to move; I couldn't see as I was blindfolded. I heard the creak of floorboards and knew that someone or something was looming over me. I could smell their breath which was strong with the smell of death. It leant over me and whispered, 'I've been waiting for you.'

NATTY STRANGE (15)
Diss High School, Diss

HOLY DEATH

'Poor Uncle George,' I sigh as I place the flowers on his grave. A storm is brewing. It starts to rain so I run into the church. I've never been here before, it's damp and quite eerie. No one else is here even though it's Sunday. I decide to wait the storm out. The thunder cracks and the church cat comes for a stroke. Suddenly, in a flash of lightning, I see a young girl! The cat hisses and when I look back all that is left is an old-fashioned doll and a pool of blood...

CHARLIE NIBLETT (11)
Diss High School, Diss

GRANDMA?

It was midnight, cold and dark. I was home with my sleeping grandma. I turned off my lamp and climbed into bed. I lay in the dark and suddenly I heard footsteps and murmuring. I gripped my duvet. I saw a shadow stretch across the landing. My body froze. 'Get out!' I thought I was imagining it, but it was really happening. I raced out of my room. Grandma was there, shaking and screaming, blood smeared across her body. I ran past her and out the house. She chased me into the woods. I screamed for help. She got me.

ROSIE LEWIS (14)
Diss High School, Diss

CHAINS

I wake up. My eyes slowly adjust to the darkness, then I realise that I'm chained to a wall. 'You're awake,' says a raspy voice. 'Welcome to my maze... of death.' The chains fall to the ground. I sprint down a corridor to the left. 'There are three paths to choose from, choose wisely, the exit is at the end of one... the other two lead to me.' I run down the middle one. I see a light. My legs are practically spinning. Then a chain wraps round my neck. 'Wrong way!' My neck snaps, I scream and die.

KIERAN BARRETT (11)
Diss High School, Diss

WAITING

Stephanie leant on the gravestone in the freezing graveyard and hoped her friend would turn up soon; he was late, as usual. 'Where was he? He could at least text, and why hadn't Mum phoned for lunch, or Dad phoned to offer me a lift home?' Were they ignoring her?
A gate clanged. Slowly, with creeping fear, she turned to look at the grave. 'Stephanie Smith, beloved daughter'. Sickened, she fled towards home but could get no further than the church. Behind her Stephanie could now see everyone else, dead like her, staring ominously forward.

KITTIE HENDERSON (16)
Diss High School, Diss

BURIED

Wind whistled through the trees outside, rousing me from my restless sleep. Disorientated, my eyes snapped open to be confronted with the unfamiliar sight of an ominous, cobweb-infested barn. I attempted to stand; my back was cold against the hard, ancient wooden floor and the feeling in my feet was seeping into the earthy void below. As my head left the freezing ground, it was forced to return by the pressure of an unknown obstruction above. I surveyed my surroundings a second time and realised I had misconstrued my setting. My barn fitted me like a glove. A coffin.

LAUREN COLMAN (16)
Diss High School, Diss

A MAN WITH AN EVIL SHADOW

It was a stormy night and the sea waves were reckless. Lenny, a fisherman, had been catching fish. He had pulled into a well lit port and he was tying up his boat. A light flickered. He heard a grunt behind him. He turned but saw only crates of dead fish. He turned his attention to his boat, but all he saw was a shadow shaped like a man. No man was visible. His boat was groaning, sinking! Suddenly, the shadow's hand lurched upwards. The captain screamed but no noise came out. The captain went down with his ship!

JOSEPH GRAYSTON (14)
Diss High School, Diss

BLACK HOWL

I'm paralysed. Am I alive? My breath hangs. Without warning,
my limbs twitch with a crippling, fiery pain. Dark rage surges
uncontrollably through my veins. It's happening.
A frenzied beat pulses against my skull. My eyes widen as they're
drowned by the midnight. They dart upwards. Out from the darkness,
the illuminated orb hangs guiltily in the sky. Always watching. Forever
silent. It did this.
Its long, silver fingers grope the edges of my trembling thighs, as I let
out a thick, blood-curdling howl.
I reach a dizzying hysteria as the delicious thought of warm flesh
caresses my new mind…

HOLLY FARTHING (17)
Diss High School, Diss

THE SHADOW

I was lost. It was my only option. The door was open and I stepped
in. It was dark when I saw the shadow out of the corner of my eye.
The door closed behind me. I took another step, then it began. The
knife entered my lower back, the pain was like no other. I could feel
the killer's cold breath on my neck. He twisted the knife and I could
feel the warm blood trickle down my legs. My lungs filled with blood
and I couldn't breathe. I fell to the ground. I was finally dead.

THOMAS PIERCE (15)
Diss High School, Diss

China Doll

Her cold, lifeless eyes are staring into mine. Her perfect china features without expression hold me, stuck where I stand...
'Genuine haunted doll,' was the description on the stand. Of course I thought it was a lie, just something to push up the price. I thought it was pretty cool so I bid and won. It arrived creepily. I placed it on my table and here I am, I cannot move. I'm hungry and thirsty. I can't look away: I am locked in its death stare. Oh God! Will anybody find me here before it is too late? Please?

EVIE NICHOLAS (14)
Diss High School, Diss

The Zombies

Midnight. Dan drove home from a party. He needed new bulbs, the lights were terrible. *Bang! Must be a pothole,* Dan thought. Suddenly, he was covered in glass as a claw punctured the windscreen and grabbed his throat, causing him to swerve off the mountain road. He stopped when he hit a fir tree. He smelt petrol. Almost unconscious and losing a lot of blood, Dan crawled from the upside-down car. Flames roared as the car exploded. Through blurred vision he saw a horrible scarred face. He crawled faster, it grabbed him. That face! The last thing Dan ever saw.

RYAN HOOK (15)
Diss High School, Diss

Footsteps

Knock, knock goes the door, followed by screaming in a field nearby soon after. This happens for four days consecutively, so the two brothers decide to investigate. On the fifth night they go through the graveyard. The gate creaks in the wind. Wolves howl. Bats fly. They reach the field through the woods. Something is following them. They hear footsteps. They squirm and look all around. Nothing to be seen. Now the footsteps are running, louder, and louder. The brothers run until they can't anymore. They are both killed in a bloody mess. He wants you...

CONNOR BLAKE (15)
Diss High School, Diss

The Whispering Hallway

I stumble into the empty house alone, darkness all around. Everyone's asleep; a sudden wave of fear washes over me, though I can't comprehend why. I've walked these halls all of my life yet now I'm on edge. There's a faint whispering. I tell myself it's just my imagination and keep walking. The whispering gets louder; I spin around but nothing's there. Louder and louder it gets with a voice I don't recognise. I freeze, paralysed with fear, feeling a stranger's warm breath on the back of my neck. He whispers, 'It's just you and me now, darling. No one.'

LAUREN SMITH (14)
Diss High School, Diss

The Figure That Kills

A girl was crawling through mud, shaking. Tears of fear covered her face. Frantically she pulled herself through the mud, sobbing into the abyss of mist. A distorted, slender face watched over. The skeletal figure approached the panic-stricken being limping forward, staggering in the knee-deep mud. The silent predator watched, its arms distorted and hands crippled like tree roots, making sounds and sharp, short grunts. Only feet away, striding towards her, slanted, twitching, as it breathed down upon her. It prized open her mouth and made an unhuman call. She followed with a sudden muffled silence.

CHARLES DAWSON (15)
Diss High School, Diss

Music Box Vs Girl

Dark. Cold. Stormy. A young girl and an imagination that runs wild. She's walking with her mum in the woods, she runs off, into the night, nowhere to be seen. A haunted house comes into her view. A box is sitting on the porch. She spins the handle and can suddenly hear cackling, deep laughing. No one is around her. The box opens, she screams but can't be heard. Gentle music is playing, wind is whistling. Alone. She cries. A voice says, 'Don't be scared, I am here now.' A man with no face takes her. Her mum shrieks.

AIMEE GARDINER (14)
Diss High School, Diss

THE FAIRGROUND OF HELL

Darkness emerged as the strobe lights flickered with fear. I was alone. They said they would meet me here. Who? That's one thing I didn't know, walking alone, dreading the unknown. I didn't know where I was going. *Bleep!* I peered down at my phone. 'Turn around' it read. I immediately felt shivers down my spine. Without thinking I ran somewhere safe... so I thought! Cradling my knees, hearing faint whispers and footsteps, I screamed internally. Laughter and cackles echoed, chainsaws roared and carnival music creepily slurred. Pain rushed through me. *Boom!* I awoke, trapped in a closed transparent box.

ANNA MARIE YVONNE ROBERTS (14)
Diss High School, Diss

THE ZOMBIE APOCALYPSE

In the deepest woods the fog was moving in and there was a crooked, old church with smashed gravestones. Jeff called, 'Come on Max.'
'I'll be there in twenty.'
Jeff went inside the church. He heard the door creak open, he thought it was Max. He turned around and it was a zombie. All of a sudden more came so he was trapped. Then, out of nowhere, Max came with a sword and knocked them down. Suddenly, he got touched by a zombie then he came towards Jeff. Suddenly he touched him so everyone was a zombie.

CAIN HARLAND-BROWN (12)
Diss High School, Diss

FROZEN FOOD

Frozen in time, the building stood just as it did twenty years ago. Outside, trolleys were still lined up neatly. Inside, food was festering on the shelf; the bones of once fresh fish had disintegrated into dust. But there was something more chilling.

Amongst the cans of beans and tomato soup tins were littered the remains of empty packets. Wheeling over to the frozen food aisle, a rounded silhouette could be seen. Crystals covered the icy remains of the fattest man I had ever seen clutching a bucket of Ben & Jerry's ice cream, spoon in his hand.

DYLAN GARDINER (12)
Diss High School, Diss

HELP!

They were getting chased, but what by? The two of them ran and came to a graveyard. They couldn't stop, they had to stick together. One fell down a hole, it turned out to be a tunnel, there was no light down there so he carried on walking and found a light. He came closer but something hit him. He fell to the ground.

He woke up and found himself in a cage, outside was a boy who looked the same as him. He went up to him and touched the boy to see if he was real...

ALANNAH MARSHALL (11)
Diss High School, Diss

THE GHOST OF THE NIGHT

Night-time noise has its own sound: An owl, a bat. Although silent I knew they were there.
I came to the gate of the church, it was open. Slowly walking amongst headstones of the dead I saw a shadow. It was no ordinary man, it was the ghost of the night. Running, I fell. Looking up towards the sky, the moon lit up his face. He killed me!
You are probably wondering how I'm telling you this, well I'm a ghost! I'm the sound in your bedroom, I'm what wakes you from your sleep. I'm the one that coming for you!

LUCY ANGELA WOODLEY (12)
Diss High School, Diss

THE BARN

At a small wood in Thetford, two children were playing. They spotted a silhouette which looked like an abandoned house; by the looks of the garden no one lived there. One child, intrigued, went to get a closer look. She could hear a faint cackling. Too scared to knock on the door, she walked over to the nearest window. To her surprise, it was her grandma! But what was she wearing? Eurghh, look at her nails! The girl could not bear one more moment, so she walked in to see exactly what was going on. Then she disappeared forever!

ELIZABETH CHARLOTTE NEWBERRY (11)
Diss High School, Diss

Shadow In The Night

I run around the corner but the shadows continue to follow. I jump into my car and head for my house. Pulling into the drive it's pitch black. I shout, 'Sam, turn on the lights. I need to speak to you. Sam? Sam? Where the hell are you?' I walk towards the door and see pumpkins. *Ha ha! Very funny,* I think to myself, he *really thinks I'm scared of this*. I stumble indoors and jump into bed. When I'm about to fall asleep I hear a door slam shut. 'Who is it?' I shout. No answer. 'Sam? Sam?'

JACOB WRIGHT (11)
Diss High School, Diss

The Spooky Graveyard

One spooky night me and Greg were bored so we asked my mum if we could go out somewhere. She said yes. We got in the car and Mum gave us some sweets to nibble on. We went to a park right next to a graveyard. My mum went while me and Greg ran to play on the slide. Suddenly, we heard a scream. We went over to the graveyard and heard another scream but it sounded different. We climbed over and then I felt a cold hand on me...

MELISSA JENNINGS (11)
Diss High School, Diss

As Death Awakens

Crash! A glass smashes to pieces. I wake up and creep out. I walk to the church. 'Bob!' I shout. It echoes through the whole church. I walk round the graveyard and I see a gravestone saying: 'Bob Charles-Talbot!' It's empty! Afterwards thick fog creeps in, I can't see a thing. The eerie noises of the creepy night-time owls scare me. I run to a gap in the fog and there is a grave with my name on it. At this point I cut my leg on a thorny branch and I see a body on the floor. 'Bob!'

JACOB HOBBS (11)
Diss High School, Diss

Spider In A Web

The light rain made the black roads glisten; thick and shiny like blood. However, through my blind, fury-following strides, I didn't notice them, nor the silent streets or inky-black sky. The adrenaline in my body burned like battery acid. I would find him there. A spider in a web where he didn't belong. I would end his crime, stop him dead. A kick to the door of my house. A battlefield of isolation surrounded the suburban fortress. 'You monster!' he understated, his body weak over my last victim. He was about to learn how all heroes suffer.

AVA WORTHINGTON (17)
Diss High School, Diss

EYES

The storm raged outside, the wind howled and the branches of the twisted tree danced with the wind. Behind the tree was a pair of glowing eyes; a glare that pierced through my body. I moved, the eyes followed me. My body began to tremble. I closed my eyes. Only the darkness could see me and my rapid breaths were all I could hear. I murmured to myself, 'It's not real, it's not real.' I opened my eyes. The storm raged on. The glowing eyes had gone. I was safe. I turned around, the eyes were looking at me...

KATIE BETTS (15)
Diss High School, Diss

THE MYSTERIOUS MANSION

The house. The one located beyond the marshes. It's rumoured to be haunted. Full of evil spirits guarding the smallest, darkest room inside; guarding the attic. Many claim that the deafening silence inside deceives those who enter, and once heard, they are never seen again. The intrigued aspect of my personality pressured me into investigating this 'supernatural' home. So off I scurried into the unknown. Walking through the wrecked, ancient entrance, I began my journey through the mysterious mansion. *Crash! It came from here,* I thought. I cautiously crept closer, to discover what was there...

CAITY ADKINS (14)
Diss High School, Diss

CANDLELIGHT

A candle, a single candle offering light to this gloomy room. I am alone. I lie on the floor, staring at the ceiling. I imagine. I dream. The candle's gone out, why? The window? A draught's coming in through the window. I didn't open the window! Icy claws crush my heart and my eyes itch with dry tears. My mouth opens but only a hoarse whimper escapes. A hand tears at the window sill and now I see an unnerving, silent silhouette skulk up the opposite wall. I pray my family finds me... Only, they don't know I'm here.

AIMEE BUCK (14)
Diss High School, Diss

THE HOUSE

I slowly opened the creaky door and stepped across the uneven stone slabs lining the floor. I looked, noticing the misfit-stained panes lie slackly in their slanted frames. I walked through a door slightly too big for its wall. I creaked up the uneven stairs, only to find myself in a long, dark hallway, lined on both sides with ill-fitting doors. A ruffled rug adorned the floor and the wind whistled softly through the gaps in the doors. I called out, 'Is anyone there?'

JACOB COLEMAN (14)
Diss High School, Diss

ALONE

Everything around you, darkness. Have you ever felt really alone? Your social security wavers as you reach for nothing. The only noise you hear is the chilling music that replays over and over, never stopping, never quitting on you. No one is around you, you think you're alone. No. No one is alone here. Your spine shivers, constant draught. Someone will always be watching you, following you. What do you really think your shadow is? Your macabre face looks in the mirror, looking for a way out. A morbid taste in your mouth as you go on alone...

EMMA HONEY (15)
Diss High School, Diss

ALONE

Alone. I loved being alone. I never talked to anyone. All I ever did at home was lock myself in my room and sit, alone, in the never-ending, all-consuming darkness. The dark made me feel safe. I believed that the darkness wasn't just lack of light, but was an empty being that waited and listened by itself, just as I do. One day, everything changed. As I sat on my bed, suddenly, I realised that that feeling of safety would never come, and I came to the conclusion that this being was near. I knew I wasn't alone.

SEM ZAAL (14)
Diss High School, Diss

Goodnight

I took my first step through my door. Then the second. Then the third. It slammed shut behind me. Trapped. Alone. I took a breath of the chilling air. They came back, the voices, thousands of them. Whispering, shouting, screaming. I stopped. I couldn't move. The voices grew louder, thumping in my ears like drums thudding in my skull. Then it went silent. Relief warmed my frozen body. It was my home again. I was free. 'You're safe,' my head told me, 'you're okay.' An icy breath hit my cheek. A cold bony hand touched my shoulder. 'Good night.'

LAUREN ARMOUR (14)
Diss High School, Diss

The Forest

The fog was creeping in, the light began to fade, my heart began to pound and my feet began to ache. Three days I spent, wandering in that dreaded forest with nothing but silence as my companion. Three days waiting for any sign of life, but what I found was far from it! Out of nowhere it just appeared in a clearing, where the full moon was shining ominously. Surveying the scene, waiting for something. I went in. I needed shelter. But all I got was fear, for this house belonged to... the Shadow!

CHARLIE CRAWFORD (14)
Diss High School, Diss

UNTITLED

As I stumbled through the dark, foggy and mysterious forest, thunder struck an old church. Light burst through the window at the top of the tower. 'Maybe someone's in there that could help me find my way home.' I knocked at the rusty old front door. No answer. I went in, not knowing what might lie in front of me. 'Argh!' What was that? Was it in or outside the church? I saw a decrepit old phone on a broken table. Without thinking, I went straight to the phone, dialling my sister's number. Something grabbed my hand! It wasn't human!

EVIE BLOOM (12)
Diss High School, Diss

STITCHED SMILES

The door creaked open and as the parents laid down their baby, they watched as she fell silent while staring into the nothingness of the dark room. That night the parents woke to the sound of rattles, they saw the child but it was peacefully slumbering. The next night they woke to the sound of tapping on the walls, once again the parents saw to the child but it was undisturbed. The third night they woke to crying and giggles, only to find the baby surrounded by dolls with stitched smiles, its lifeless body was limp in their arms.

TEGAN KERRY (13)
Diss High School, Diss

Chased By The Living Dead

I was strolling out of school one day, feeling delightful until a blood-curdling scream pierced into my ears and then another and another. I ran back into school; it felt eerie with a strange atmosphere. That's when I felt breath running down my neck. Not just one person, more like a hundred. I steadily rotated my head and my life flashed before my eyes. Standing there I saw over two hundred zombies. I bolted out of the classroom door, anxiously screaming for help. I was not fast enough, I was caught by the crowd and never seen again...

Ellie Moore (12)
Diss High School, Diss

Untitled

It was a stormy night and everyone was trapped outside. The houses were all destroyed and everything else was destroyed by the lightning. None of the people knew what to do, except for this one man who knew what to do. He said that he would use his powers and try to save the world, but then the lightning got even worse and killed him and everyone else. The people who did all of that stuff were actually aliens.

Adam Wyatt (12)
Diss High School, Diss

THE STORY OF THE UNKNOWN

I heard it rambling in my garage. What was it? What was there? I quickly grabbed my torch. I held it to my chest tightly. I was scared! I admit it, I was really scared! I'd just got home from school, it was already dark. I slowly walked out of my house, I forgot that there was a step so I nearly fell over but I didn't. I walked through the stable and finally got to the garage, we have five of them. I saw someone. 'Who's there?' I asked.
'I am the unknown!'

CHARLA ANN RULE (11)
Fakenham Academy, Fakenham

THE CAT WITH NO NAME

Night fell above our house, my dad left to go to work before I saw him. I was meant to be asleep. But I couldn't. There was a scratching sound at the back of my head, screams gathered overriding my thoughts. Then it came alive. The terrifying screeching screams pierced through my door. I rushed to my feet, heart thumping faster than a train. I ran and opened the door to my living room. I looked to find only scratches of her left. Dead. Nothing. Just a small cat with no name sitting. Staring. Then it left, disappeared... gone. Forgotten.

AMBER SMITH (13)
Framingham Earl High School, Norwich

THE REVENGE OF CELSTIA SNOW...

'Prim, come and see this!' Gale whispered through the woods that my mum, Katniss Everdeen, hunted in. I wandered over to the lake, when I got there Gale clamped his hand over my mouth to stop me from screaming. I saw peacekeepers building trucks and guns, but I thought the war was over. The Hunger Games was over! Was this Celestia, Snow's granddaughter, plotting revenge? We both ran towards the hollow tree. Me holding my bow, I grabbed the sheath. I knew how to shoot straight but it was too late! They'd seen us! What should I do? Oh help!

ABBY SCHOFIELD (11)
Framingham Earl High School, Norwich

HER SCREAMS ECHO

The hallway stretches in front of me. The door, reveals a crack. There's a girl crying. I edge towards the door. She stops crying. I lay my hand on the door. I'm shaking so much I don't need to put any force into pushing it. I can see her, she's hugging her knees. I take one step into the blackened room when, the girl looks up at me, her face stained with blood. She stares at me. Something grabs her hair. She screams bloody murder as she's dragged away. She digs her nails into the floor. Her screams echo. Echo.

AMBER JOHNSON
Framingham Earl High School, Norwich

CLOCK STRIKES MIDNIGHT

The clock struck midnight as Lindsay was heading home from a party. She received an anonymous phone call, she answered, 'Hello?' The phone hung up. She could hear footsteps, she started running. The footsteps got louder. She finally stopped and looked behind her. It was a man wearing a mask. She saw a rock in his hand. He ran at her, she let out a huge scream as he hit her round the head with a rock. She looked up with blood pouring down her face. He dragged her body into an alleyway and strangled her to death painfully. 'Daughter?'

JOSHUA HEWITT (13)
Framingham Earl High School, Norwich

DEATH WAS ONLY THE BEGINNING

Death, was staring me in the face. The wind howled chillingly through the leaves. I had no choice, I had to enter. Screams! Every instinct I had wanted me to stop in my tracks. As the mist rose, bodies covered in blood emerged from the darkness. They drifted towards me as their eyes pierced my soul. I felt a cold breath on my neck. I turned, twisting my frozen body. My name rang out of his mouth. The creepy ghosts echoed my name. I ran, but it was too late. They had entangled me. But death, was only the beginning.

LIVIA PETTIT (13)
Framingham Earl High School, Norwich

Church Of The Dead

The church stood on top of the large hill. Megan was climbing up the hill, she eventually reached the church. Megan walked into the church, it was cold and damp and stank of dead bodies. Cobwebs hung from the ceiling, the wind was howling. *Bang!* There was a sudden noise. Megan froze solid, she didn't know what to do. It was pitch-black apart from one candle flickering. Suddenly, the door opened. Megan could faintly see a black figure. She didn't know who it was. She thought maybe the vicar but not at this time of night. Who could it be?

Jessica Quinlisk
Framingham Earl High School, Norwich

Danger

I entered the deserted forest which was silenced by the gleaming moon. I didn't know what laid behind each tree I passed. Nor did I know danger lurked beneath the deep depths of the forest that night. Crispy leaves rustled on the ground waiting for me to stumble over them. Trees stood tall, sending cascading leaves down to the forest's floor. Danger lurked beneath the deep depths of the forest that night. It felt like someone was watching me. Howling wind was deafening me. Leaves were clutching me. Oh danger lurked beneath the deep depths of the forest that night!

Oscar Albrow (11)
Framingham Earl High School, Norwich

Don't Let Him In

Water dripped through the broken roof. As I lay there, all life's troubles stood in front of me. Whilst I was drowning my sorrows with vodka, I heard a knock at the door. *Who could it be at this time of night,* I thought to myself? 'Hello,' I called after an absence at the door, still nothing. I assumed it was a couple of kids looking for trouble. At least, that's what I thought. As I turned away suddenly the door flung open but there was no one there. I was scared. That's when I realised no, he was there...

Ben Harding (14)
Framingham Earl High School, Norwich

The House

We walked into the house. Suddenly there was a creak coming from upstairs, the others followed. 'This is not a good idea,' said Thomas. Poppy just ignored him.
As soon as they got to the top step Jessie screamed. 'Jessie what's wrong?' said Poppy turning round. But Jessie wasn't there. 'Come on, let's go upstairs,' said Poppy.
Poppy began to walk upstairs. As soon as they reached the bedroom door there was another scream. 'Be quiet Thomas!' said Poppy, turning round again but Thomas was nowhere to be seen and Poppy was never seen again.

Iona McKie (11)
Framingham Earl High School, Norwich

Falling

A young lady stood in her nightgown, her skin pale and fingernails drumming against the cool wood of her kitchen table. 'He said he'd be here by now,' she said into her mobile.
'He'll get to you soon.'
'I guess,' she sighed. 'Anyway, I need to go, I'm really tired.' The receiver clicked silent. She felt cool air on the back of her neck. Turning around, she saw the window was open. Walking with a cold sweat on her forehead, she went to close it. She felt hands on her back, and all too quickly she was falling.

HANNAH DYE (14)
Framingham Earl High School, Norwich

The Door That Creaked

Every night when I was young I shut my door and I went to sleep. I would wake up in the middle of the night from my door slamming, it made a loud bang. Every night I would go and check what it was and then, one night, it didn't happen but I did wake up because I needed the toilet. I was in the toilet and my bedroom door slammed. I went to my bedroom to see what it was and I went in to find my grandmother dead. I was so scared.

LIAM CLEMINSON (13)
Framingham Earl High School, Norwich

Alone

'Hurry up!' I groan as Daniel begs me to follow him to an abandoned old cabin. We trudge along. We get to the cabin and open the door to go inside. A voice mutters. A trapdoor appears on the dusty floor and my legs carry me forward. I try to get Daniel to help, but he's gone. My foot goes over the edge and I'm falling. I land on something grimy and horrible. It's dark and there's no sign of Daniel. I'm surrounded with cannibal mutants. I'm completely alone...

BENJAMIN SEAMAN (11)
Framingham Earl High School, Norwich

Face The Fear

I entered the dimly lit hall after hearing a piercing scream so loud it felt like my ears were bleeding! As I turned around a basketball bounced across the floor and a clockwork doll with one eye sprinted across the ground. Suddenly, the clock struck 00:00 and another scream shattered the silence. I was walking in circles, struggling to breathe. All of a sudden a window opened and there, sat on the steps, was a clown holding a balloon, blood running down its face. I felt a hand on my shoulder. This time it was me screaming! Fear! Danger! Death!

AMELIA CROPLEY (12)
Framingham Earl High School, Norwich

DEAD DREAMS

Running, I embraced the wind brushing against my face and blowing my hair back. Suddenly I heard screams as loud as sirens but as chilling as ice. I approached with caution; I pulled the bushes away revealing a horrifying sight. Three dead bodies laying helplessly as blood trickled from their necks onto crippled leaves. I accelerated away, the bushes rustled and then a growl! I discovered an abandoned house and made a dash for it. I clutched the frozen doorknob, the stench of blood was overwhelming. Then a chilling claw touched my neck, fear rushed to my heart.

HAYDEN SUMMERFIELD (12)
Framingham Earl High School, Norwich

THE FREAKY FOREST

I went to a friend's house, and I needed to cut through a forest so I did. I suddenly heard a snap. 'I think it was just a stick,' I said to reassure myself. Then I heard an owl and I got very scared, so I just started to walk quickly to get there. Then I tripped and felt a fluffy thing in-front of me. I quickly got my bag off my back and got out my torch, then it died, the batteries were dead. I felt it and then I felt eight legs. It was a…

AMEYA BILL-ETESON (11)
Framingham Earl High School, Norwich

It Wasn't Me After All

I walk towards the house, the curtains are closed and the window is wide open. I open the door, it is unlocked. I hear strange noises coming from inside, but I still walk in. I feel something on my shoulder and when I turn around I see nobody in the moonlit night. I think it's just me being sensitive. I walk one step and close the door behind me. I see a shadow, no surely it's just me messing with my head. I'm scared. I scream for help but it's too late, I've been shot. It wasn't me.

Hattie Mae Ebbage (11)
Framingham Earl High School, Norwich

A Nightmare

It was a dark, windy night, all I could hear was the wind blowing and the wolves howling as I approached the forest. It started to thunder. I shivered but carried on. As I got deeper into the forest I saw a tent. I went into the tent and it turned out to be a circus. I stopped and listened, I heard something round the back. I peeked round the corner and saw a gang of clowns. One of them spotted me. I ran as fast as I could. Suddenly I woke up in a daze. It was a dream.

Megan Benson (11)
Framingham Earl High School, Norwich

NIGHT TERROR!

I stumble in, desperate to get away from the blizzard. I sit down and get my phone out. The seats are very dusty. There is an eerie silence but it feels like someone is there, looking at me. *Pat!* Someone's there. My heart is racing one thousand beats per minute. I try to run but the door has disappeared! I am running, hoping not to be caught. I can't get away. I hear grunting. Suddenly a hand grabs me and I'm on the floor! I see its face....
I wake up and I feel normal. I was just dreaming, wow!

ZAK HOUGHTON (11)
Framingham Earl High School, Norwich

THE HEADLESS HORSEMAN

The stone floor was frozen as I tried to sneak towards the mossy spire. Slamming the door shut I attempted to call my brother, Ross, but my phone had mysteriously vanished from my pocket. The smell of rotting flesh came from the steps above. Walking closer towards the top of the spire, I noticed a jade light on the stone wall. Feeling further up the wall, I came across a glass window, shattered glass surrounded my feet as I stared at the midnight sky. Cold breathing pricked up the hairs on the back of my head. I turned around. *Bang!*

MAX NOBBS (12)
Framingham Earl High School, Norwich

THE FOREST

As I'm walking through the empty, pitch-black forest I hear the twigs behind me snap. I suddenly look behind me, as I look I see a shadow sprint past me. I start running, not even knowing where I'm going. My heart's pounding, blood rushing through my body. I reach in my pocket to grab my phone but I have no service. As I'm running I look behind me and see a man with a mask on, all I can see is his bright eyes staring at me. He starts walking towards me quicker and quicker. His hand grabs me...

GEORGIA RAYNER (12)
Framingham Earl High School, Norwich

THE SHADOWS OF EVIL

I woke up. There was a drinks machine next to me. I got some Juggernog. It suddenly occurred to me there were three other people around me and all wondering the same thing, 'What is that noise?' I walked up to a window with bars on. The noise was getting closer and the smell, well smellier. We suddenly noticed a box in the corner of the street which looked like an octopus, it opened and a pistol shot out of it into my hand. A zombie came round the corner. I loaded my gun. Time to kick some butt...

DYLAN HALL (12)
Framingham Earl High School, Norwich

Cursed Love

I was coming out the school gates and I saw the sign saying: *Road Closed!* That meant for me to get home I had to walk through the forest. When I got into the forest it was silent. I looked up and everything was still. There was a small path so I followed it. Out of the corner of my eye I spotted a man with a black hoodie covering his face. I turned around and he was running after me. I started running as fast as I could but he caught me. He pushed me to the ground...

Alice-Mary Bowman (12)
Framingham Earl High School, Norwich

The Chase

As I entered the room faint screams entered my ears, slamming lockers shook the walls and a voice sang, 'La la, I've got your mother, your father, your sister, now you!' I swung my head round, not knowing what lurked around the corner. Gloom filled the air. My heart stopped for a second. I ran, ran like my life depended on it because it did. Through classrooms, weaving between tables, I turned, stumbling to the ground! The clown! His red hair, black eyes and white face made me shiver to the bone with fear! He ran towards me and grabbed...

Lily Dimmock (11)
Framingham Earl High School, Norwich

The Lost Temple

It was very foggy, I couldn't see. It was too dark. I could hear murmuring, someone else must be here! 'Help!' I shouted into the distance. Nobody answered. There was a red light flickering in my face. 'I think I'm in a temple!' Suddenly, a shadow appeared. It looked like a man, but then, I looked up. It was a mummy! I ran through the tunnel, it was following me. I came to a dead end. There was a button on the wall. *What can it do?* I thought to myself. I pressed it. Then, I saw the light...

Owen Page (12)
Framingham Earl High School, Norwich

Wasteland

I woke up. The start of a new world, all I could smell was meat as I opened the window. I walked out the front door to my garage and drove down the road, only to see this figure staring at me with blood dripping off its face. I drove back home to my garage and went down to the basement, I grabbed my flamethrower and got in my truck. I went down the main road and there was a swarm of them all walking to the same place. I looked back and there was more, they came at me...

Elliot James Martin (13)
Framingham Earl High School, Norwich

Shadows

I'm walking through the streets in the thunder and rain. Running towards an alley for shelter, I can feel myself breathing heavier, heart racing. Shadows creep up on me, I turn around, *bang!* The shadows are growing taller, towering over me. I run and find myself in an abandoned church. All I remember is the door opening by itself. I sit on an old dusty chair in the corner of the room. Grey and miserable I rethink what has happened. The door opens. 'Hello?' I'm shaking with fear all over. I can't look back, I feel breathing on my neck...

ELLA SMALLS (12)
Framingham Earl High School, Norwich

The Opposite Of All Horror Films

There were four of us, we stayed together. After that we heard a noise from the basement. We went downstairs and realised the basement was open, so we avoided it. Then we went into the town centre and saw a dark man walking into a shop, I didn't follow him. He then ran out of the shop with a chainsaw and tried to kill us. So we ran and the sexy but dumb cheerleader tripped over nothing and wouldn't get up. She screamed for help but then got killed. There was a car that started, so we escaped.

DANIEL NEAL (13)
Framingham Earl High School, Norwich

THE SHIVERS

It started chasing me. As the cold air slapped my cheeks, I sprinted through the dark woods. Every leaf crunched beneath me. Every inhale burned my lungs as they filled with frozen air. It was getting closer as I dodged each tree. My aching side growing stronger. Pain shooting up my legs as I tripped. I felt the blood burning my head. It was over. It ripped me open as the zombie dug its hand into my guts. I screamed as I saw my intestines in front of me, being crunched and chewed in its mouth. Was this the end?

JENNIFER MURDOCH (13)
Framingham Earl High School, Norwich

THE LAST ONE

I am the last one. The world was destroyed by greed and the need for global power. My whole family. Gone. Everyone I loved. Gone. I felt like someone was constantly watching me. I wasn't prepared for it. I couldn't ever have been prepared. There was a knock on my door. My body froze, a whistling noise pierced my ears, overriding all my senses. Creaking and screaming everywhere. I couldn't hear; my heart was pounding in my ears. The hairs on the back of my neck tingled and then I realised the door was open. I wasn't the last one...

MARTHA WHITE (13)
Framingham Earl High School, Norwich

The Shadow

I felt a fear descend down my face. What was behind the door? I started to run. My breath getting heavier and heavier. My leg was bleeding badly but I ran on. There were footsteps coming closer and closer. My head was burning. I panicked. I curled into a ball, crying loudly, almost screaming it was so loud. *Snap!* A stick cracked. The shadow was closing in on me. I was too scared to look up. I stared at the floor and I knew I was going to die. What could I do? This was the end of it all.

Xanthe Conway (12)
Framingham Earl High School, Norwich

Paranoia

It started with rain, then the thunderous storm raged on. It's been going on for weeks, but I must venture on. The twisted pavements are soggy and messy. I've got to get back, I have to, home's the only safe place left. They're coming for me, now they're standing outside my house. Wait, I can go in Mother's cellar. She said not to go in but I have to. As I enter, an eerie fog clears, I shudder. A book lays in front of me. Pandora catches me, I read the book. Everything changes. I'm stuck here, or am I?

Finley Evans (13)
Framingham Earl High School, Norwich

THE UNDEAD

Running, I can't stop, not after what just happened. Jack and I were in the damp, dead forest when we heard a bang followed by a scream. We crept forward, trying not to be seen. That's when I fell into the deep cave. 'Hello?' I call out. I feel the water soaking through my old, blue converse. Footsteps, out of the shadow steps a faceless man carrying a gun, dragging a body. All I can think is run. 'Jack?' I breathe, no answer. 'Casey is that you?' I trip and fall, *bang!* I scramble to my feet. 'Jack, you there?'

MATHILDA NOTLEY (12)
Framingham Earl High School, Norwich

DARKNESS

Darkness. The reigning darkness is over me. As I'm in this bleak veil of mystery fear consumes me; I can't breathe. My time's precious. The walls are closing in on me and I'm trapped in an impregnable location. Solemnly, I try to get up, Alas, I'm chained up and I can't escape. The wind moans at me as if saying everything is my fault. My crypt illuminates because of the shadowing lightning through the tiny hole. *Crack!* The darkness intensifies and again the burden gets heavier. In my final moments the stench of decay fills the air. I hear it!

EDWARD JAMES WILSON (11)
Framingham Earl High School, Norwich

The House In The Woods

As we wandered through the woods we came across a mansion. I thought we could break in. We entered the house, we yelled, 'Hello?' No answer. I wandered upstairs, the bannister was soggy and wet and the smell was unbearable. We searched for some food in the grand kitchen. We found some tinned beans but we could not get the hob to work. So we ate cold beans for dinner. Afterwards, we were very exhausted so we found the main bedroom. As we lay, the power went out but the phone rang, and a cold hand touched my foot. 'Dan!'

ALEXANDER DANN (12)
Framingham Earl High School, Norwich

The House Of Shadows

Abandoned house in the middle of the woods, it was dark. The girl walked in, there were lots of bats festering in the house. Her heart was pounding. She knocked on the door, it flung open. As she felt a hand on her shoulder, she shivered. She stepped in and wiped her hands down her shirt because of all the orange rust staining her hand. The dust filled the room, she started to cough. Her eyes watered but she was okay. She carried on walking but then an old man ran through her. She looked behind her, there was nothing.

ELEANOR RICHES-HOWES (12)
Framingham Earl High School, Norwich

THE BUTCHER

Colin ran through the gnarled trees. He stumbled and saw an old house. He sprinted towards it. He fumbled with the rusty doorknob and could smell foul breath and rotting flesh. Colin ran into the house and slammed the door. He glimpsed a fat butcher with a bloodstained apron and a meat cleaver. Colin ran upstairs, into the bathroom, and locked the door. He heard footsteps thudding up the stairs. He could smell the butcher's foul breath. Then the footsteps creaked on the floorboards outside the bathroom. Colin heard the lock clicking and the door slowly swung open...

JACOB RUSH (12)
Framingham Earl High School, Norwich

A TALE OF TWO TRIBES

In the Northern mountains of Kalimor lies two tribes, the Goshmog tribe is full of Urgals and the Kudumban tribe is filled with Kull. These two tribes have been at unease for a millennia, until now none has declared war. It comes from nowhere. A band of berserk Urgals appear in the Kull Chieftain's camp. They burn it all and kill the chief and chieftess, leaving their son an orphan. Now their vengeful ghosts stalk Kalimor, taking pleasure in the torture of others. They slowly rip out the victim's guts and eat them. Then they leave them to the hounds...

THOMAS ROSE
Framingham Earl High School, Norwich

HE GOT ME

It was dark, so dark, then I opened my eyes and I saw nothing. I blinked a couple of times and still nothing. I went to the power generator in the basement. I turned it on and got myself a drink but the tap was left on. I was the only one home. I turned the tap off and heard someone or something running down to the basement. Then the power went out and there was silence… a deafening silence. I rushed to the basement to turn the power on. As I ran I hit hard spikes. He got me!

JAMES CUNNINGHAM (14)
Framingham Earl High School, Norwich

WITH ONE TOUCH

'Here's our new house, Joe,' mentioned Joe's mum.
'Yay,' Joe responded sarcastically.
'Do you want to look around?'
'Sure, bye.' The village was dull and nothing was happening until I found an old, unused house. I opened the creaky door and went in. There was a doll on the stairs with a knife in her hand, and to my left was a clown and to my right were people trying to kill me.
The doll said, 'Finally, after all these years, someone to kill!' I screamed, then they screamed. They were dead and, with one touch, so was I.

ARWEN ELISE GIVEN (12)
Framingham Earl High School, Norwich

THE CABIN

Ben and I finally agreed with the old man that we would clear his cabin for £100! 'I think we'll buy a lot of sweets.'
'This seems easy!' exclaimed Ben.
As we walked into the dusty surroundings of the old man's wooden shack, I looked at a sign that said: *Watch Out Wendigo About!* 'What's that?' asked Ben.
'Just some old man's junk!' I said. I put my hand on a balcony and suddenly I fell off the balcony, into a mineshaft. Ben screamed so I climbed back up. He was on the floor with a man decapitating him. *Cannibal.*

DANIEL LILLEY
Framingham Earl High School, Norwich

CAN YOU SURVIVE THE HOUSE?

I reached for the door. Of course, I did. I couldn't resist a building which looked like it could crumble down at any moment. The door began to creak open. The only thing that I heard was the ferocious wind hitting nearby trees but another noise started. It sounded like a girl weeping and singing 'ring-a-ring o' roses, a pocketful of ashes, a-tissue, a-tissue they all fall dead!' The girl stopped crying immediately and began laughing, but a chill travelled down my spine. All I could see was sudden darkness as though I was dead.

AMI EDWARDS (14)
Hellesdon High School, Norwich

BREATH OF LIFE

She stumbled through the damp, dim caverns, shuddering as she passed chains loitering ominously above, as if they were getting ready for an ambush. She should really be used to it now, but unease still seeped into her very bones. She skidded to an abrupt halt. The piercing hissing and blood-curdling wails had faded to a silence pulsing like the heartbeat of a slumbering child. She'd done it; her freedom was only a few steps ahead. She flinched when a shadow stained the wall like ink. 'What are you doing?' he sneered. 'Looking for a breath of life,' for evermore.

SAMAR AROHA KIANI (13)
Hellesdon High School, Norwich

ASPHYXIATED

Imagine you're deep underwater with no sense of freedom for being submerged in total darkness. What would you do? Would you keep swimming and just hope you're going up? What else could I do? With my heart racing, the tank isn't reassuring. Swimming, desperate for light. I freeze suddenly; instinct warning me to look round and I catch the oxygen tank on my back, the bubbles leaking into the ocean. My heart stops. I exhale but am overcome with trepidation, seconds before seething pain rips through my skin; lungs compressed, screaming for no one as I'm slowly dragged into oblivion.

CHARLOTTE ROPER (14)
Hellesdon High School, Norwich

THE UPRISING

Aaron sat by the graveyard slowly reading the newest issue of the Walking Dead comics, he felt like the King of the Undead. The darkness crawled in slowly like a plague of evil. The street lights came on one by one with only flickers of light like candles in the wind. He walked home, the infected had risen. Aaron managed to reach home once, to see his brother and sister consuming his mother and father's brains, tearing and ripping as if they were sloppy mash potatoes. Aaron froze as zombies piled in, clawing into the insidious brain within…

CHANDLER ELLIS (14)
Hellesdon High School, Norwich

THE LAST NIGHT SHE LIVED

Lucy opened the graveyard gate cautiously but unaware. The bright surface of the moon was full, crows squawked endlessly as a warning. The wind started blowing as violent as a tornado. She heard a voice. 'Lucy,' it said. She panicked. 'Lucy,' it said again. 'I can see you.' Lucy started running towards the chapel. She pushed herself up against the statue. 'You can't escape me.' She turned around and saw a figure with a bloody axe. Lucy screamed as the thunder and lightning roared. The shadow man sliced his axe down. All was black, not a sound was heard.

AMBER ELLIS (12)
Hellesdon High School, Norwich

The Dream That Wasn't A Dream

It was a dark night, Lyra came across an old door. Her curiosity led her inside. She found a corridor. She entered but with every floorboard that creaked, she edged closer to doom. There was a dark room and a broken camera, suddenly, twins came onto the cracked screen. 'Come play, Lyra.' She dropped the camera and screamed. Suddenly, a silhouette of a man holding a gun appeared before her...

Bang! She woke up, it was a dream. Scared, she reached under her bed for her teddy. What she saw next made her realise, it wasn't a dream at all.

ABBIE GREEN (11)
Hellesdon High School, Norwich

Broken Skin

What's that you hear? The haunting screams of your wife? They echo as you hurry down the muddy road. The wooden door swings open, unveiling your mangled wife. Crimson tears flow down her newly broken skin, slowly slipping away from you. A shock-filled wave hits you. You fall to your knees, grabbing hold of her. Hair falls from her face. Trembling, you press your lips against hers. Warmth and cold mix, unreacting. 'It's my fault, my love,' she whispers. Confused, you stare at her. She smiles.

'One second too late,' it giggles.

SHELBY CAROLL (14)
King Edward VII Academy, King's Lynn

THE RAVEN'S SCREAM

Locked inside with no way out, running from the raven and its scream as it echoed down the hallways, chasing us no matter which way we turned. The walls were watching us and slowly closing in. I shrieked as a chill ran up my spine and the sound of the raven's scream became louder, penetrating my eardrums. I stopped at the sound of my sister begging for her life. I ran in every direction to find her but I did not succeed. The passages were long, narrow and too similar for me to find my way, I'd lost all hope.

KATIE BUNTING (14)
King Edward VII Academy, King's Lynn

WINK MURDER

The teenagers sat in a rough circle and peered into each other's eyes, waiting for someone to wink. Sophie's black hair cascaded down her back, her dark eyes stabbed through her opponents. She winked once at Ava and she fell to the ground. She winked again at Rowen, he fell to the ground. She winked at Ivy, she fell to the ground, along with the others. The room fell into silence, Sophie slowly looked down at the ground and her hair gently fell down her shoulder. She smiled as she knew that the friends were never to wake up.

RUBY DIXON (13)
King Edward VII Academy, King's Lynn

The Strange Adventure

One day, in the damp forest, there were many people trembling past this unknown, mysterious creature. No one realised it was lurking there, until it pounced at any of its innocent victims. This creature was one-of-a-kind, a mysterious creature that didn't like people or sound. As soon as someone came past this monster it would strike and you'd hear an ear-piercing scream emerge from the mossy, green woodland. Even though anyone could hear this sound, no one would bother to come and help the poor innocent victim! This would be the last time it struck!

Ellie Bower (13)
King Edward VII Academy, King's Lynn

Spirit Train

Walking along the train tracks, I knew I was alone in this world. I just felt so empty, I knew I had to leave. Yet, I felt so happy, knowing I'd finally escaped the trauma of life. I could do my own thing from now on, with nobody to tell me otherwise. I turned around. The train was coming straight for me. I braced myself for the impact, closed my eyes and smiled to myself. The impact never came. But it was okay. That same train had already hit me once before.

Mia King (14)
King Edward VII Academy, King's Lynn

THE HIKE TO DEATH

It was raining heavily, but Lindsey still wanted to hike. I warned her not to. I even said, 'She's stupid!' But I loved her. We'd been married for a year. Oh my gosh, she was wrong. However, she talked me round. I couldn't let her hike alone, it was too dangerous. We set off. Of course she chose the slipperiest path. We were climbing extremely high. It was slippery, windy and raining. We were at the highest peak. She raced forward. That's when I heard her bellowing shriek. I ran, looked down and saw her lying at the bottom, dead!

KATELYN HALL (14)
King Edward VII Academy, King's Lynn

LIFELESS KNOCK

It was getting late, I was alone, I dawdled up the creaky stairs to get ready for bed, when I heard a knock at the door. I opened it, no one was there. A second knock. Was I going mad? Or, was it reality? This time I didn't answer. The door opened, a flow of eerie mist blew into the only room with no lights. I jumped at first until a force dragged me into the dark room. I fell to the floor and laid lifeless.
I awoke to find blood everywhere. I soon realised I was dead!

OLIVIA ROSE SHARP (12)
King Edward VII Academy, King's Lynn

THE LONELY HOUSE

The lonely house stood still, its walls crumbling away. Moss had grown in-between the cracks and up the walls. Flowers surrounded the house. The sound of birds fluttering away filled the desolate meadow. I rested in the lonely house. The once beautiful home was now no more than a dark building in shambles, illuminated by the faint moonlight that seeped in through the cracks. As my eyes began to close, I saw a figure out of the corner of my eye. The gloomy figure watched - sending a shiver down my spine. I left, looking again at the lonely house.

SAMANTA STRAUTA (13)
King Edward VII Academy, King's Lynn

THE LAST GLANCE

It was the 10th December 2008, Mum was unable to sleep, Dad was pacing up and down the hallway. We knew things were not right. As morning dawned upon us, there was a strange feeling of uncertainty that lingered around. Mum was pale, unable to withhold her pain. Every few seconds she would glance up to the left corner of her bed, I found it somewhat unnatural. There was something there. I looked a final time, the colour drained from my face. Mum had been taken! Who by? Her name was Maia; she had her next helpless victim lined up…

BRIONY BENJAMIN (14)
King Edward VII Academy, King's Lynn

77

THE REFLECTION MAN

Today's the day when I start moving all my belongings into my new house. It was an early Christmas present from my mum and dad. Finally, I sit down and watch TV. Suddenly, the TV comes up with the silhouette of a man who has broken out of jail. Looking outside my glass door, I see the silhouette of the person. Running to the phone I call the police. Glancing back at the door and he's closer but there's no footprints in the snow. The phone drops and I realise it was a reflection of the man behind me.

JOSEPH CLUNAN (13)
King Edward VII Academy, King's Lynn

THE DESOLATE GRAVE

The church seemed bright and welcoming; a grand and beautiful building compared to the flats surrounding it. The wind rustled the leaves and whistled through the church grounds. Lottie had always thought it weirdly calming. She'd only recently arrived and was seated beside her mother's grave. It was becoming dark and she started to feel uncomfortable. She'd never stayed until dark so decided to see what it was like. Lottie sat still, her eyes closed, thinking of her mother as she always did. She heard a scream beside her ear and quickly stood, her heart hammering in her chest. 'Help!'

MORGAN CHIPPERFIELD (13)
King Edward VII Academy, King's Lynn

Untitled

'Where are we going?' I asked her. No reply. I looked at Willow, she looked as crept out as I was. Annabeth had been in an odd mood all day, but now she was seriously worrying me. We tiptoed down the ancient staircase and entered the main hall. Moonlight streamed in the ornate windows, casting tall shadows that danced around us. 'OK, we're here, what now?' I asked Annabeth. Silence. Then suddenly there was a creak and bang! The door locked. We were trapped. I whirled round. Her feet lifted off the ground. She raised her head and screamed...

SINEAD ALICE MARRAY-WOODS (14)
King Edward VII Academy, King's Lynn

The Legs

In the freezing kitchen I've picked up the shiny knife and have stuck it down near the shut door to see what's on the other side of the door. All I can see are four legs, it seems two different people are standing there. I call Tom from the other side of the kitchen to have a look. When Tom makes his first movement the legs are moving about in the same area. The people on the other side start to knock on the kitchen doors, shouting in their creepy voices, 'Open up!' Tom gazes at me with fear…

KRISTINE LEBEDEVA (14)
King Edward VII Academy, King's Lynn

NIGHTMARES ARE REAL

When Ruth Jones' alarm clock woke her at seven o'clock that morning, she had no idea that today would be the longest day of her life. When her alarm clock woke her she wasn't in her bed, she was not in her living room but she was on an old dentist's chair in a dark room. The room smelt of burning hair; personally she didn't like the smell. It felt like she had a migraine, she looked to her right to find all her hair on fire on a tray. She said, 'Nightmares are real, it's real.'

HARRY CHANDLER (13)
King Edward VII Academy, King's Lynn

THE FIERY PAST

The flames grew, darkened and furiously chased the girl through the black, oak woods. She fell over a small trunk, snapping her ankle. The fire got closer, burning everything in its path. It filled the air with a deadly breeze of grey dust, killing the birds above. The girl limped her way to a tree, breaking every inch of hope in her soul. She stopped, gave up and passed out. A bright light shone on her face. A black blur stood in front of her sore body. The young girl survived only with a scary story to tell her tale.

LUCY SCHOFIELD (14)
King Edward VII Academy, King's Lynn

Good Thing You Didn't Turn The Lights On

I'm returning from a party. I open the door to mine and my sister's room. I don't turn the light on so I won't wake her up. I step into the room and close the door. I get into my bed and fall asleep. I awake in the night with an uneasy feeling. I creep up and turn the lights on. I scream instantly, calculating what I'm seeing. Red writing on the wall saying: 'Good thing you didn't turn the lights on'. In the corner of my eye I see my sister laying on the ground. She was killed.

Katrina Borovika (13)
King Edward VII Academy, King's Lynn

Watching Over

Annie woke up in her cold, empty room, but she couldn't remember why it was empty. She ran out of the house, missing breakfast and sprinted to school. When she arrived at school all of her friends ignored her for some reason. When the bell rang, her friends left to go somewhere but they didn't invite her. She followed them as they went to the cemetery! Annie shouted but they didn't answer. They eventually approached a grave and laid some beautiful flowers. Annie cautiously read the tombstone which said: 'Annie Willson 1998-2014'. It was her grave!

Alice Middleton-Jones (13)
King Edward VII Academy, King's Lynn

Miracles And Cheer

It was a Christmas like any other; the whole family came to our house for the week. It was cold outside so we stayed inside and played games we found in our basement. We didn't use it much, maybe because we were scared, we couldn't describe our fear.
On Christmas Eve we ran out of games. Fearfully I went to the basement by myself to see if there was anything to keep us company. We found something called Efil Ruoy, it was a big, colourful box and was a card and dice game. The game decided all our lives.

GABRIEL DEACON
King Edward VII Academy, King's Lynn

Trapped!

Tiptoeing into the foggy, abandoned graveyard, I shivered. Wailing came from every grave, 'H-hello?' I said stuttering between my every breath. Running towards the gate something grabbed my leg, I kicked to get free. Thankfully I got to the gate, pushed it but it was locked! 'I'm trapped!' Slowly turning around I saw hands shooting from every grave. Sprinting over them I aimed for the church. Nobody was there. I crept between the pews to get to the top of the church to see if anyone else was there. 'Hello?' Weeping with relief I got to the altar. 'Hello child.'

TALIA JANE HOLLISTER
Litcham School, King's Lynn

THE HOUSE

I walked through the old, rusty garden gates and looked around. Then I glanced at the flowers in thousands of rows as black as night. They were drooped over, crying as their petals fell to the ground, realising that their lives were ending. I turned around wondering if I should go home, but I didn't, so I went up to the big, oak, wooden door. I looked up at the house as it towered over me like it was waiting for me to go in. I went in without thinking to knock! Then, *bang!* Then, *click!* I was trapped.

AMELIA GOLDSBY (11)
Litcham School, King's Lynn

STALKED IN THE WOODS

I always liked going for walks in the wood, it was calm and helped me escape from the troubles of life, but one day haunts me forever... The day was cold and misty so you couldn't see too far ahead or behind. The crunching from when I stepped on the leaves started to get louder but I took no notice. When I stopped I could still hear the crunching. I thought that it was an animal until I heard a quiet laugh. I turned round and a man lunged at me! I ran away and never went back!

JACK RABY (11)
Litcham School, King's Lynn

TRAPPED

I clutched the doorknob, hoping it would be open. The door opened with ease so I took a large step into the entrance. I smelt a strong, musty smell. An ancient rug sat moulding in the doorway. I saw a red substance on the floor, making me feel uneasy. My hands coiled around the bannister. I felt a suspicious presence with me as I roamed the empty corridors alone. I crept into what looked like a bedroom and sat down for a break. All of a sudden the door slammed shut behind me. I was trapped. Alone. Forever.

TARA ROBYN BECK (11)
Litcham School, King's Lynn

THE MANSION

It was eleven o'clock on Halloween Night. The night was one of the darkest ever. I was walking in a forest when I found a large, hidden mansion. Like all curious people I went inside. The doors slammed shut behind me. I tried to force the doors open again but they wouldn't budge. I walked down the hallway looking for an exit or staircase when I heard a noise. It was a girl laughing. I tracked the noise down to its source. The sound was coming from a room. The wallpaper was torn down, leaving behind the terrifying world. 'Run!'

CALEB BOWER (11)
Litcham School, King's Lynn

THE FRIGHTENING FRIDAY

One Friday evening I went for a walk. It was getting darker and darker. At 9 o'clock I had to go back but it was only 6 o'clock. I saw an old house, it looked like nobody lived there but I wasn't sure so went in. The door was unlocked. I looked around for a while until I saw a figure walk downstairs. I was freaked out but went upstairs, where all the activity was happening. I looked outside but couldn't see because there was a face. I ran for my life as I was absolutely freaked out. Finally home.

DYLAN FRYETT (11)
Litcham School, King's Lynn

TIME WILL PASS

It's been seven years since Mother died. She said to me before she went, 'Don't go near the house. It's number 13,' then she went. Finally, I think I'm going to investigate that house. As I walk down the cold, empty street I feel the nerves as I approach the house. I walk in. Is that what I think it is? The house is coloured green and it has a lot of dust and cobwebs. As I approach the stairs I feel uncomfortable... then, *bang!* I fall dead on the floor and, reader, I advise you: don't go there.

HENRIQUE ALVES (11)
Litcham School, King's Lynn

THE DARKNESS AWAITS

Darkness fell on the deserted street. Thick fog swirled around me, dampening my dark grey coat. I needed to get away from home, with all the arguing and everything. I just needed some 'me' time, quiet and peaceful. My feet dragged heavily along the gravel street, towering trees blocked out my view of the twinkling stars above. The skyscraper-like trees seemed like figures watching me. I stopped dead in my tracks as I heard a faint sobbing. I strolled over to the child who sobbed and warily patted her arm in reassurance. Ice-cold I collapsed, eyes fluttering shut.

ADA EVERETT (12)
Litcham School, King's Lynn

IT CAME FROM THE WALLS

It all started when Dad was working on the electrics. He dug into the wall to try and mend a light switch, he heard a growl and then a rumble. Next thing we knew we heard a scream, it came from upstairs. We ran to my sister Allysia's room. When I opened the door we saw a completely empty room with a note reading: 'Playtime'. We were all terrified. We all split up to search the house. I was in my room alone when I heard footsteps approaching from behind my door. 'A-Allysia is that you?'
'No!'
'Please don't! Argh!'

CHARLES CROOK (11)
Litcham School, King's Lynn

THE TRAPPED FOOTSTEPS

The gravel crunched under my feet and I stopped to look around. I saw a white flash out of the corner of my eye. I ignored it and moved on towards the door. Beside the door were two oddly symmetrical arrangements of weeds and both had ivy that climbed up the walls, meeting at a point and making a cross shape. The towering house drew in a breath and its blood rushed around in the form of water and pipes. Pushing open the oak door, the house shivered and the door abruptly slammed shut behind me. I was trapped here.

MILLIE FISHER (11)
Litcham School, King's Lynn

THE HOUSE

It was dark and the fog was getting thicker. There was no one to been seen but there was a house, shadowed and mysterious. The gate was covered in ivy and very stiff. In the garden it was completely overgrown with weeds. I stepped onto the gravel, it crunched like bits of bones breaking. There was a figure, transparent and menacing. The curtains were flying out of an open window like they were trying to escape. I dragged my feet to the front door. The knocker was made of brass. I bashed the door with it. The door opened…

SOPHIE STANGROOM (12)
Litcham School, King's Lynn

THE LOFT!

The soft ladder groans as I pull it down. The chill from the attic meets my face. I shiver without warning. The smell of an autumn forest fills my nostrils as the damp tumbles downward, mixing with the odour of rotting timbers and stagnant air. My enthusiasm to find my box of old photos drains away as I carefully climb the narrow treads. I strain to see as I reach the top; years of dust cling to the light bulb making it too dim to be of much use. Suddenly I hear a bang behind an old painting; I'm terrified…

OLIVIA CHARLOTTE RUBY MCCARTHY (12)
Litcham School, King's Lynn

IT WAS A DARK NIGHT

It was dark and gloomy. No one was around, not a single person to be heard. I was lost and didn't know how to get back home. I could see an old, dark castle with a light on inside. I thought if I could get to the castle I could maybe get directions home. There was one problem: the door was locked. I tried pushing the door open but it wouldn't move. Suddenly, the door mysteriously swung open so I walked in. I walked in and turned around to see a ghostly figure shut the door behind me, then ran.

GRACIE ENGLEFIELD (12)
Litcham School, King's Lynn

THE ROCKING CHAIR

After I slammed the doors behind me, a huge dust cloud rose from the shattered floorboards filling the air with dusty fumes. There was only one door that led to one candlelit room. Inside that room there was an ancient rocking chair. The rocking chair rocked gently but there was no windows for the wind to blow the chair. The chair started to blow vigorously, a blue light shone around the decaying frame. I screamed for my parents but nobody could hear me. Something tapped me on my shoulder. Then everything blacked out. Was it just a bad dream?

DANIELLE MIA HARROWING (11)
Litcham School, King's Lynn

THE GHOST

I think I was supposed to be asleep but I couldn't, all those silly ghost stories had scared me and Mum and Dad were in France. Clara, my older sister, had to come to stay for a couple of days. No way was I going to that bossy boots for help with anything! *Bang!* What was that? I heard myself scream Clara's name. 'Shut up!' she shouted back. I hid under my quilt. Could I hear movement downstairs? My mind raced, wondering what it was. Could it just be the people next door? Why were the noises getting closer…?

CHARLOTTE BOYLE (11)
Litcham School, King's Lynn

My Night Shift At Henry's

I once worked at a family restaurant called Henry's Farmyard. It was a nice place with nice people. There were animatronics too. Some people had terrifying nightmares of them because they looked like weird animal human hybrids. There was a night shift. Sometimes, when people do the night shift they never come back to the restaurant because they quit instantly. Nobody knows why they quit. It's probably because the animatronics move in the dark, including the old ones. Tonight was my night to look over them but one was in the hallway. Its head was twitching like crazy.

Matthew Brown (13)
Litcham School, King's Lynn

The Abandoned Factory

One day three teenage boys were going to the park to hang out. On their way they saw an abandoned factory, so the three boys entered. It had no lights inside, it was pitch-black. A boy pulled his phone out and put the phone torch on. It lit up the whole place. They could see a hole in the floor. They looked inside the hole and could see something white shining. They could only make out that it was a skull of a human. Suddenly, one boy felt an icy-cold hand touch his shoulder!

Max Casey (11)
Litcham School, King's Lynn

THE THING IN THE NIGHT

I ran as fast as I could. He was following me, I was sure of it. I saw an old shack and ducked inside. It was cold, dark and smelt funny. What was that banging noise? Something moved in the darkness. I looked around but nobody was there. 'Hello?' I whispered. 'Anyone there?' No reply came. I moved further into the darkness. The leaves rustled around my feet and the wind howled. That was when I saw it riding in the wind. How had it found me? I had no answer but to run. This was it. Charge!

REBECCA TUCKWELL (13)
Litcham School, King's Lynn

THE LAST GOAL

It was a lovely warm day in California, the sun was shining and the flowers blossoming. I was playing football with my friend, James. I was winning 2-1 and I had the ball. I dribbled up to the penalty box. I shot but James the keeper made a wonderful save in the top right-hand corner. He threw it out and I got the ball again. I was running with the ball up to the halfway line when I remembered that my best friend James, the boy that I had always been with, had died awfully two whole years ago.

ALEC CHALMERS (11)
Litcham School, King's Lynn

NIGHTMARE OF MOONGLOW SWAMP

As I trembled out of the warmth of my house I heard something. 'Hello? Who's there?' I tried to speak but all that came out was a whisper. For some reason I went into the swamp, Moonglow Swamp. Rumour has it that it is haunted by ghosts. I took one step into the swamp and I instantly felt cold. 'Come closer.' A voice drifted on the air. *Thud!* My tiptoeing sounded like stomps. *Thud!* Then I realised it wasn't me. I heard an eerie sound behind me. My heart pounded furiously. I turned around but nothing was there. *Thud! Thud!*

LUCY ORR (11)
Litcham School, King's Lynn

A NIGHT AT MY STEP-PARENTS'

A night, at my step-parents', is a horrible experience because my step-parents are bad to me. But one day it all changed. I was sleeping in my cold, damp bed when I saw the light from the hallway spilling out into my room. It was very late at night and my step-parents were out. I climbed out of my bed, crept to the door and opened it to look out into the bare hallway. A door opened and heavy breathing came out from the silence. The breathing became more raspy and heavy until I reached the door. Silence.

FRED FOULKES (11)
Litcham School, King's Lynn

A PALE FACE

Pulling myself up from the dusty path, I found I was in a garden with dead and withered plants everywhere. At the top of the garden was an abandoned mansion which suddenly lit up with lightning. In shock of the flash I was thrown back to the floor, then I felt cold hands planting themselves on my shoulders and hoisting me back up to my feet. Trembling with fear I slowly turned around, though saw nothing but an endless garden. Perplexed, I turned to face the mansion and saw something that terrified me horrifically: a pale face in the window.

LIBERTY BLACKMORE (11)
Litcham School, King's Lynn

UNRAVELLED

I walked up a stony pathway, up to an abandoned building. The moonlight shone down through the thick mist and the gentle wind made the leaves rustle. I looked ahead. On the door of the crumbling building was a note tied around the steel handle. As I unravelled the shrivelled piece of paper, I started to get suspicious. In bold red writing it said: 'This way, I've been waiting'. I opened the wooden door and stepped inside. The candles were flickering on the wall, making shadows and patterns on the cold, stone floor. Suddenly, I was in total darkness.

LEAH GIBSON
Litcham School, King's Lynn

The Lab

The knives and tools were half illuminated by the moonshine through the open window. The Professor was halfway through his revolutionary reincarnation experiment. He placed a creepy looking toad onto the table and started to run electricity through it, until it dropped down dead on the table.

A few minutes later the toad sprung back to life but it looked like a cockroach. It then proceeded to scuttle off the table and onto the floor. The Professor then realised that he had successfully reincarnated a living thing. He then laughed in a sadistic manner.

Joe Knights
Litcham School, King's Lynn

The Monster

Once, there was a man who was interested in almost anything scary. He had recently found an ancient cave in South America but he didn't know the cave was haunted. He was going to investigate it today with some mates. They entered the cave and, almost as soon as they walked in, three of the five men went missing! The man was petrified, he had never seen such a horrifying thing in front of him. It looked like an enormous… well, he didn't know what it was. The thing hadn't noticed him. He slowly crept away. The monster turned…

Ben Casey (13)
Litcham School, King's Lynn

UNIDENTIFIED

Walking alone at midnight, down an isolated street, is never a good idea; trust me, I should know. It had started as an ordinary day, I'd been at school, boring as usual, had dinner at home and ended up at my friend Danny's house. Pretty normal so far, but what followed me home will never leave me. Bushes swayed but, strangely, there was no wind. At the time I assumed it was a coincidence. A shadow appeared in front of me. Was it Danny? I cried out his name. There was no answer. I turned around; nothing to be seen...

KIAN DESMEDT (11)
Litcham School, King's Lynn

COLD FINGERS

Drako's feet scraped along the sidewalk as he paced around the church walls. The inky darkness made it hard to see. As he made his way to the gates, Drako could feel icy-cold fingers stroke his arm. He shivered. Something was watching him. The gates slowly opened and he froze! Drako stepped tentatively forward towards the church doors. There was no wind but suddenly they opened. He ran into the church but couldn't see anything, then stumbled over an object at his feet. It was a silver dagger. The cold fingers seemed to push him forward. Drako's heart stopped…

SEB BATES (11)
Litcham School, King's Lynn

HORRIFYING HOUSE

One misty, thundery, chokey night I walked past the house that I walk past every day to get home from Cubs. Something had changed about the house though because the curtains were never shut. You could normally see the wrecked rooms in the house. I was very suspicious of the gross house when something moved in the rushes of the deserted garden. I went to have a look in the house, avoiding the rushes. The door creaked shut. I had a feeling I was being watched. Then the bell struck five. Ghosts came up and said, 'They're coming.'

RILEY ROBINSON (11)
Litcham School, King's Lynn

WHEN I RAN AWAY

I ran away. I came to an old bridge with a tall carved oak door with holes in it. I edged closer towards it, wondering what was going to happen next. Thinking, *what is on the other side?* Bad thoughts sprung into my mind about death and Hell. I touched the handle tightly with my hand and pushed down slowly and gently, opening it until it was ajar. I peeked through. I saw an eye stare right back at me. I swung open the door but nothing was there, nothing but a sharp drop.

ISABELLE TAWANA (13)
Litcham School, King's Lynn

The Shadow

The wooden door closes as a shadow walks past. You remember that this also happened to you last week and you don't know what to think. Your mind goes blank and then you hear the door creak open. Your heart starts to beat faster and faster. The door looks like a prison and it feels like you are trapped inside the room. The dark blue curtain blows into the shadow's face. The figure leans over you and breathes over your bright red face. The breath stinks of cat biscuits. The figure says, 'I know what happened.'

HANNAH CANNELL (11)
Litcham School, King's Lynn

The Haunted Doll

I walked over to the abandoned, broken house where the old woman used to live. I stumbled my way through the debris on the porch. The handle was cold and stiff. The door opened without a push and, as soon as I lay a foot inside, it closed behind me. Paralysed in fear I felt a presence. Too scared to turn around, I ran into the room on the left and slammed the door. Inside was an old rocking chair but nobody was causing it to rock. I took a step closer and a doll sharply glared at me...

SOPHIA LOUISE DJIAKOURIS (12)
Litcham School, King's Lynn

I See Dead People

This is a story I have never told before. I went to visit my grandma's house for the weekend. My grandma lives in an old house. I knocked on the door. My grandma said, 'Come in.' I went in and she said that I can stay in the spare room. I unpacked my stuff, looked out the window and I saw a ghost.

My grandma came up and I said, 'I can see dead people.'
Grandma looked out and said, 'I can't.'
'It's coming in the house.'
Later on I went upstairs, it was there in my room...

Molly Bunning (11)
Litcham School, King's Lynn

The Night

Back in 1945 World War Two had ended and there was a huge party that the whole of England was invited to. Everyone went except a boy called Billy who stayed home to play with his black kitten. At 11.50 Billy heard a bang from upstairs, he ran upstairs to see a chair race across his room. He quickly ran back downstairs, something was there, a deathly face flew at him. *Dong, dong, dong, dong, dong, dong, dong, dong, dong, dong, dong, dong,* the clock struck midnight and then there was silence. His parents came back and saw something ghostly...

Jack Colwell (12)
Litcham School, King's Lynn

HAUNTED CHURCH

The fog was closing in on me. I couldn't see anything. I took hold of an old, rusty church handle before realising the door was locked. I was alone. My friend, John, was in the church. I found a pile of rubble by the side of the church. There was a hole that led right into the church. It was like a secret passageway. For a moment I was scared, yet excited. I scrambled through the secret passageway and froze in the cold, silent atmosphere. A cold, pale hand came up behind me and touched my shoulder. 'Hello.'

CHLOE WHITMORE
Litcham School, King's Lynn

NO LAND

Trembling, I crossed the border into No-Land. The thin ice and frosty snow freezing below, the base of my feet, my toes frozen. Blood turned blue in my icy body. I glimpsed up and saw a dark figure shining, like it was an angel guiding me some place. I tried to run to the figure but my legs were walking in a slower pace, than ever. No-Land was the coldest place on Earth. No one came back alive, they couldn't come back or tell the stories of what they saw. It was only me who dared to be alive.

ROSIE CHANDLER (12)
Litcham School, King's Lynn

THE LITTLE IVY COTTAGE

I was weaving in and out between trees, slipping and sliding in the mud. My heart was racing, I could hear it thumping in my head. I could hear its footsteps behind me, getting closer by the second. I stumbled upon a little run-down cottage covered in ivy. The door was hanging off its hinges, so I stepped inside. It was covered in cobwebs; cold, dark and damp. I ran up the stairs. There were dead bodies tied to the bannister. I went into a room as I heard the monster's footsteps. It came closer. Then it went black.

LOUISE CLARKE (12)
Litcham School, King's Lynn

UNTITLED

There had been lots of reports about a haunted hospital, so eventually the police went to investigate. When they entered they started to hear some calls from an old phone. They picked it up and a frightening voice said, 'Welcome to my hospital. I have brought you here to hear my plans. Firstly, you must kill one from your group. You have one minute to do so or you will all die. Good luck.' Immediately, one of them picked up the radio and the commander said, *'Get out. The calls are coming from inside the hospital! Get out!'*

REUBEN ALMOG (12)
Litcham School, King's Lynn

THE CLOWN

A shiver ran down my spine as I felt the cold metal of the door handle. When I stepped in there was nothing but old toys in the shop. Dolls with eyes missing, a wind-up music box and... a clown. Two foot tall and with a grim smile on its face. I looked further on, into the rundown toy store. Everything had been destroyed! Wherever I went, I felt like I was being followed or watched. Then I turned around. It had moved. The clown was behind me, reaching out to grab me with its deadly grin.

TOM SPENCER (11)
Litcham School, King's Lynn

WHAT WAS IT?

The dark was creeping in, I could've made it back before it was too late. I was stopped in my tracks by a thick fog. I came across an old house with a light on so I went in, thinking that I had found safety. There was no one there except for an old couch that had been layered with dust. 'Hello?' No answer. Silence but for my own voice which had anxiety in it. Carefully, I laid down. I must have been asleep because the light was switched off. At that moment a cold hand reached for me...

SIMON BIRD (11)
Litcham School, King's Lynn

MYSTERIOUS MAN

I was walking down a road when I saw a man. His skin was pale but he was covered in a thick layer of a dark, dusty mist. The clothes he wore were black all over, parts of what looked like a designer jacket were peeling and he had jeans that were massively ripped. The air surrounding him tasted bitter and charred with the wreaking smell of burnt food. Not even when he was walking did he make a single sound, the only thing I could hear was the sound of wind behind him. He was a ghost.

SCARLETT STEVENS (11)
Litcham School, King's Lynn

OUT OF MY DEPTH

I felt a twisted knot of fear as the dark closed in around me. I could see the thick fog building up on the surface. Gulping for air, my lungs filled to the brim with water. I was sinking... I kicked my legs as hard as I could, trying to get to the top. It was no use; my usually lightweight body had now become immobile. Ice gripped my lungs as I tried to make sense of what was happening. Through the confusion, I heard someone calling my name....

KATIE ANNA DUTHIE (11)
Litcham School, King's Lynn

THE OLD PARK...

I looked up. Dark shadowy clouds were caving down. Soon it would be dark. I looked back sharply. Not one of my school friends were in view. With fear I chose to take the different route. The route that was always empty! An eerie feeling that someone was following me rang in my mind. Obviously this was my imagination. The park which always seemed a safe place was coming up. *I'll stop there,* I thought. As I pushed the creaky gate, I realised *I'm not alone*. As I turned around a slender figure followed me into the park. 'Hello…?'

IZZY TABOR (11)
Litcham School, King's Lynn

THE GHOST AND THE MIRROR

There was a mirror, no ordinary mirror. A man walked in, looked at the mirror and saw a ghost. I turned round, there was nothing there. The next day I woke up and I couldn't move, I couldn't scream, I was helpless. I felt a chill go down my spine. I saw a white orb emerge from my chest. I couldn't move. I just realised that I'd been possessed. Later I thought to myself, *this has been the worst day of my life.* My vision was changing, it was changing into a red tinted vision. I stabbed myself.

OLIVER BOUCHERON (11)
Litcham School, King's Lynn

Bella And The Tracks

One day on a cold winter's night, as the rain began to pour and the thunder clashed, Bella began to walk along the rusted, moulding train tracks, flashing her torch on. The sight around her was pitch-black with only the trees looking like people that might kidnap her. Slipping over the tracks she hit her head and she fell. Soon she became unconscious and started to roll down into a chasm. Bella soon woke, wiping the leaves from her face and held her head. Bella shot up as she saw people grabbing her. Screaming. Nobody could hear!

Erin Lawes (12)
Litcham School, King's Lynn

No Escape

Blood trickled down the man's crumpled face. His head was spinning, he had to keep going. He walked heavily, hunched over, dragging his feet. Then, in the pearl-white moonlight he saw the outline of a big house! He crawled to the front door, all life seeping out of his body. The wide, oak door slowly creaked open but there, facing the old man, reappeared the apparition. Its eyes were red like burning coals, full of hatred. It stretched out its sharp talons round the man's thin neck and squeezed until the only sound to be heard was the wailing wind.

Evelyn Scott (11)
Litcham School, King's Lynn

ASYLUM

I stared up at the old building. The sign clearly said: *Asylum, Do Not Enter!* But I knew I had to; Joe was still inside. I pushed through the broken, rusty wire to find the door hanging open on its silver hinges. I ventured in and let the door fall behind me.
A few hours later, I still hadn't found Joe and was about to give up when I heard laughter. A mad cackle echoed down the halls. Something grabbed me and I just managed to croak, 'This isn't funny Joe, let go of me!' The thing just cackled again…

GEORGINA DENNEY (12)
Litcham School, King's Lynn

THE ORPHANAGE

I was looking for somewhere to stay for one night as my car had broken down. I came across an orphanage. It was abandoned by the looks of it but that was fine. I walked in, well, had to break my way in. I walked around with the bitter aroma of rotten blood left in the old canteen. I could hear the cane cracking. It sounded as sharp as knives. I could hear a girl laughing in a room. I walked in, still hearing the continuous laughing. I went into a room with a fire. She laughed and screamed.

DOMINIC HANCOCK BOGGUST (11)
Litcham School, King's Lynn

THE EYE

I'd finally given up running from it, once I'd figured out it only marks my soul. The fact is, this demonic symbol appears when I need it to. It might set alight a path on the floor showing me home or scare off the imminent bullying ritual for a week or hopefully more. The thing is that it burns through me. I mean literally burns through my bones as if a chainsaw into a sapling. I've already lost a finger, a toe and a tooth. It doesn't hurt but it's constantly bleeding. I'm drowning in it. Now that's a curse.

FINLEY BARNES (11)
Litcham School, King's Lynn

THE STRANDED HOUSE

The house stood alone as the door creaked open. Full of hatred I stumbled in. Broken windows and the smell of burning blood drifted past my nose, making me feel cold and scared. Thick dust flew up into the empty space in front of me. As I took a step forward, the house growled. My fingers twitched, my feet went numb and all I could feel was the empty room closing in on me. The walls were cracked, the carpet was ripped and the windows were smashed all around me. Then I heard the key twist. I was trapped!

AIMEE WRIGHT (11)
Litcham School, King's Lynn

THE SHADOW DOG

There I was, standing in the alley. Scanning the ground in the darkness for a small, silver key. I heard snarling behind me! A sensation of ice-cold pins ran down my spine. I could hear hard claws against the cobbled path, getting closer and closer! Having heard tales of the shadow dog I spun around, its glowing red eyes stared into my soul! For a second I was paralysed with fear and then I made the decision to run to the nearest door! As I ran I could hear its heavy feet behind me! *Thud! Thud! Thud!* I stumbled…

TURAYA HAMMOND (12)
Litcham School, King's Lynn

THE FORGOTTEN SOULS

The wind began to pick up. An ice-cold chill trickled down my frosty spine. As the fog started to clear I spotted an old, abandoned cottage. Almost frightened to death I raced over to it. Rusty and mouldy, the door handle lay there on the dead floorboards. The walls were covered in thick layers of dust. The whole place was filled with icy air that froze my fingers and toes. I found a rotting stool to sit on. It was black and wet. There was a blanket on the floor. I covered myself with it. *Bang!* The door opened.

ISAAC BOWER (11)
Litcham School, King's Lynn

Abandoned Cottage

I woke with a start to find that it was still night, bitter cold, with only the man in the moon to watch over me. The dark haunted me, I could feel its cold breath on my shoulder. An unusual scent of death drifted past and a pale sound of owls squawking. I edged forward, watching my every step. I looked up to find myself in front of an old abandoned cottage. It was the past and present. Gnawed at every corner, the door handle felt cold. I walked in. It was dark and bare, nothing but empty space.

ELLA WESTHORPE (11)
Litcham School, King's Lynn

My Friend Jim

Once, there was a doll that lived in a wooden house. I watched people go in and a hearse come out. I was staying around my friend's house. My friend is known as the village's superstitious person because he believes in ghosts and people becoming alive again. As normal he was talking about ghosts and I was not paying attention until he mentioned the house where the doll lived. He said last weekend someone went in there and did not come out. Then he said, 'Let's go in there.' I disagreed as I watched him go in there...

ELEANOR ASPINALL (12)
Litcham School, King's Lynn

Vampire By Night

On the 14th of June 2015 I woke up from a slight chill down the back of my neck. I looked around and thought, *what was that?* I got out of bed and went to the bathroom. 'Argh!' I cried. 'Someone's dead and a man is drinking her blood!' I leapt back, grabbed my crucifix and told the man, 'Be gone!' The man screeched and fled like a bird leaving the nest. I went up to the woman. She woke up, but with mighty long fangs.

The next night, *bang!* The woman was banging on my door so I fled…

Matthew Maddox (12)
Litcham School, King's Lynn

Cats Aren't The Only Ones Who Die From Curiosity

Jamie's sister had been missing for almost a week and there were still no clues on her disappearance. Jamie thought about this as he walked to school. He had gone mad about finding her, so much so that his friends had lost him and teachers stopped trying to help. He didn't know who his parents were and his foster carer was away. As Jamie reached the front gate of school he felt a cold breath on the back of his neck. At that moment Jamie realised that maybe he didn't want to know who his real parents were.

Daisy N I Wood (13)
Litcham School, King's Lynn

It

It was a stormy night as I trekked through the forest. I was tired, plus my clothes were drenched, so I decided to take shelter in the abandoned shack up ahead. I stepped inside. It was cold and unpleasant. When I turned around I realised how vast it was. The walls were lined with tools. I saw a switch on the opposite wall and stumbled towards it, bones aching. I flicked the switch but nothing happened. It was then I felt the hand and saw it. The ripped clothes, the mangled face, the slender knife…

RYAN BRAMLEY (12)
Long Stratton High School, Norwich

The Knock

I couldn't sleep, the wind was blowing. I tried to block out all the noises around me. I tried putting a pillow over my head and tucking myself in but I still couldn't sleep. I had a fear that I couldn't get out of my mind. I heard Mum and Dad breathing heavily. There was a sudden knock at the door. I heard Mum and Dad slowly move downstairs, yawning. They opened the door, I heard two people fall to the floor, I started to panic. I heard footsteps slowly coming towards me. I stopped breathing. This was the end.

EMILY BELL (12)
Long Stratton High School, Norwich

THE TWO CARCASSES

On a lonely night a wolf howled through the darkening trees. A little boy stood shivering in terror at the bloodstained rocks. The carcass lay next to it, ripped. The murderer sat behind the hedge, waiting to pounce. Pouncing, he thrust the dagger into the boy. As he fell the wolf let out a howl. The two carcasses lay together, side by side. As the murderer walked away he cackled and knew the job was done.

MEGAN GROOM (11)
Long Stratton High School, Norwich

DANCE ALL OVER

Rose once went dancing and she was having the best time of her life. She was in the middle of her dance, not realising anything. Suddenly, everyone else vanished, but not her. What had happened? She turned around… There was a man standing in black, holding a knife and sword. 'Wh-wha-what have I d-done?' She started running, but he followed. Then… *stab, stab, stab!* Rose started falling, dead, not alive. What could she have done? The man started dragging her out of the building, into the trees where nobody could find her. What was going to happen?

ALANA MARTIN (11)
Long Stratton High School, Norwich

GRAVEYARD DEATH

The creaky gate squeaks as I walk in the graveyard, the trees rustling, the wind howling! I feel a shiver go down my neck, there's someone else here as well! I turn, cold, scared, a shadow whizzes past me, I hear a grrr! Then, something pulls me; grabs my legs. I am pulled down a hole, never to be seen again!
Every night someone comes to the graveyard looking for me; every night someone is haunted by my curse! And, if I'm angry someone gets what happened to me... They die! Anyone who steps foot in my graveyard gets it!

ALISHA JERMY (11)
Long Stratton High School, Norwich

THE BOY WITH THE BLOODY NIGHTMARE!

Lights on! Lights off! Flickering in the dark. A young boy with a bloody nightmare! The clown in a jumpsuit, the one with the knife and the luminous red Afro! Waking up, the boy hears a noise and creeps into the bathroom... Bloodstains are up the wall and written on the mirror is: 'Mummy!' Suddenly his dream comes to life, a clown appears and grabs him around the throat, holding his knife up. To the boy's terror he says, 'Your mummy's dead!' The boy screams and the clown slits the boy's throat, then his arm and then his stomach...

SUMMER WHITING (12)
Long Stratton High School, Norwich

IN THE TREES

This happened about two years ago, it still freaks me out when I think of it.

I was walking with my two friends. We'd just finished fishing and it was getting late. We were halfway towards my van when I saw a strange man run from the side of my van into the woods. I screamed into the woods with anger. We were almost out of the woods when we saw the same man, but this time he was dumping an old body in a body bag into the river. I've never been to the woods since it happened.

HARRY PETER BARBER (11)
Long Stratton High School, Norwich

THE STRANGER

One dark night there was a boy called Damian Bloor, he was walking home from the park when suddenly... *bang!* There was a gunshot, Damian felt as if he had been stabbed in the back. He fell into a puddle of his own blood. As he lay dying a strange figure leant over him and said quietly, 'I'm sorry but you've ruined my life once, I'm not letting you do it again.' And with that he left Damian Bloor on the floor and was never seen again. The stranger is still out there so be very careful.

CHLOE OLIVER (11)
Long Stratton High School, Norwich

A Prank?

Once, on a dark and gloomy night, someone called Greg was in his mansion, but there was a smash from downstairs. He turned the lights on, they didn't turn on. Greg slowly walked downstairs with his phone light on. He got very worried because he heard whispers. Greg looked around the door. No key. Greg tiptoed through his house. The lights flickered. Greg fell back in shock. There was a man with a mask, in a suit. The lights turned on and Greg's friends jumped out laughing… It was a scary and frightening prank. Was it?

COBY MOORE (11)
Long Stratton High School, Norwich

Demon With The Black Horses

It was dark and damp in my old cottage bedroom. I could hear my parents snoring in the next room and the tapping of the rain on the roof. Suddenly, the rain stopped, everything was silent when a sound of galloping horses and the cackle of a man. I stumbled across my room, trying to avoid the clothes on my floor. Out of the window I could see him riding across the field. He stopped. He looked up at me with his daring eyes. Next thing I realised was that I was tumbling. Immediately I landed on the floor lifeless.

RHIANNON DYKE (11)
Long Stratton High School, Norwich

ARE YOU DEAD OR ALIVE?

It was a sunny day when there were no dangers on the beach until one day Roy went swimming and started drowning. He looked down and died. Jeffery, James and Jeremy got in their boats to get Roy's dead corpse. They looked around only to find James had been eaten by a shark and the boat was sinking. Jeremy fell in and was eaten by a bigger shark. Jeremy ended up surrounded by great white sharks. He felt half eaten alive, he wasn't sure if he was dead or alive. He was dead, surrounded by sea creatures. Nobody is alive on Earth.

JOSH HOWARD (12)
Long Stratton High School, Norwich

KRUMPUS

It was Christmas Eve and everyone was sleeping all through the house, but one unfortunate Christmas Eve Alfie was awoken, he wandered downstairs to discover his beloved auntie was being held in the clutches of a mythical creature they call Krumpus. He ate Alfie's auntie right in front of him, then he grabbed Alfie. He squirmed, shrieked, kicked and punched until Krumpus let him go. He bolted to the basement where he hid in some crates. He could hear the beast wander downstairs and open the crates, until he found Alfie… Will he survive this Christmas?

CHARLOTTE ELIZABETH ROCHESTER (11)
Long Stratton High School, Norwich

THE BUTCHER

One night in the butcher's shop I heard a scream. I hid under my pillow, I looked out of the window and saw a light from the butcher's cellar where he keeps the meat. The light was yellow, then turned red. At first I was scared then my neighbours went and knocked on the door. He answered, I closed my eyes and they were gone, I hoped they went home but the next morning some kids went in and never came back out.
The next day I was watching others go in but never come out again.

DAMIAN MOORE
Long Stratton High School, Norwich

THE HUNTERS

One day, on a dark rainy day, a girl called Lucy went to the city with her mum. There was only two or three people in the city. The lights went off, it was so dark she could only see lightning. She heard screaming, the lights turned on. There was blood and guts on the floor. She screamed and ran out of the city. She ran to a spooky churchyard to speak to her father. 'I don't know where Mum has gone. I need you, please come back,' she cried. She looked beside her, 'Mummy don't die, please.'

SKYE SHREEVE (11)
Long Stratton High School, Norwich

THE PARCEL

One evening, there was a little family, who lived in a little village called Hempnall. It was cold but they went for a walk and it was incredibly dark. The wind was whistling and the wind was getting louder and louder so they went home. The TV was on and then they couldn't find the little girl and the news said there's a murderer around in Hempnall, so they thought she was dead. The dad went to look for her but he couldn't find her so he went home.
In the morning a parcel came... It was her chopped up.

POPPY FRANKLIN
Long Stratton High School, Norwich

THE DEAD GIRL WALKING

In 1873 there was a girl called Claudia. When she was nine a shadow man came into her room. Suddenly, *bang!* She was… dead! Today in 2015 on Halloween Night she will rise from the grave. At 11pm Claudia was here. Claudia started to walk down the path and everyone who strolled by, she scared them so much they ran down to their parents screaming and crying, but there was a boy called Tom who didn't run away from her.
A few days later Tom and Claudia fell in love. Then Tom died to be with Claudia.

KIRSTY OGDEN (11)
Long Stratton High School, Norwich

THE LOST CHILD

As the fog comes in I'm starting to get scared. Finally I find a church.
I go in. It drops suddenly, it feels like I'm going into a mine. I can see.
What is that? I think it is diamonds. I'm in joy, can't believe it. Then the
cart suddenly drops straight down to never be seen again.
Well thirty years had past, not a single murmur until exactly
November 1934 Friday 13th, a gunshot, only one. It had been on the
news for about a week. Now what happened. We wait, never to hear
the gunshot ever again…

ARCHIE FISHER (12)
Long Stratton High School, Norwich

THE MAD SCIENTIST

On a stormy night, in an abandoned mansion, in a graveyard the
mad scientist was about to do something terribly wrong. The night
the thunderstorm hit was when it began. The night after the storm
the mad one started to get the components he needed to create the
monster! First he got the jaws of a tiger. Then the neck of a giraffe
and then the legs of a tarantula and the DNA of a chameleon and
also the ability to swim.
The next day… 'Yes, yes, I have done it. It's alive! Time for revenge!'

THOMAS PAYNE (11)
Long Stratton High School, Norwich

THE HOUSE

One stormy Halloween Night, Kate and I walked along the dry, cracked path on Lakehouse Drive. The mist in the air gloomed in front of the glowing full moon. The moon hung like a medal above the old wooden house on the hill where the apparent ghost of the last owner haunts. Kate suggested going in, we did. The door had paint peeling off. It creaked and a cool, breezy gust of icy air hit us. The stained furniture was ripped. As we walked, blood oozed out of the walls. A faint scream. Kate! Suddenly a gloved hand grabbed me…

HETTY MERCHANT (12)
Long Stratton High School, Norwich

GHOSTLY

'Are we nearly there?' asked Amile.
'Shut up,' I said.
'Yes Ammi, don't be so rude Jamilia.' That's when we arrived. Me and Amile went straight down to the beach. We were playing in the sea when I saw him. I shouted over to him but he just disappeared. I screamed. Amile was stumbling up the beach, entranced. He walked into a cave and vanished. I followed him. I found him by an altar with the ghost. Suddenly, his spirit left his body and entered the ghost. I screamed again. Then I fell to the floor. That's all I remember.

MILLIE BARNES (11)
Long Stratton High School, Norwich

BLOOD!

I stood in the churchyard, in the darkness. I wore all black, my hair flowing down my back. It was cold. I walked slowly through the graves. I heard gunshots in the distance, they sounded close. Shivering, I didn't know where to go or what to do. 'Come here,' a creepy voice whispered. I turned my head, left to right, up and down. I felt something touch my shoulder. I stood still. A hand crept over my mouth. I didn't move, the hand was cold and soft. Fog was around my feet. A knife slit my throat. Blood poured everywhere.

BETHANIE AUTUMN SCOTHERN (11)
Long Stratton High School, Norwich

MY JACKET

Darkness was upon me, I was already late home. A door opened and a gentle woman appeared. She removed my jacket and explained the situation via phone to my parents and that I would stay the night at hers. So in the morning I left, accidently leaving my jacket. My parents informed me to retrieve it. I arrived to find a man. No woman! Apparently the man's wife died years ago. He took me to her grave. 'Marjorie Elwin died 3rd August 2010'. My eye caught a glimpse of my jacket just sitting upon the grave waiting for me...

ISOBELLE HOWARD (11)
Long Stratton High School, Norwich

THE UNWANTED VISITOR

There was a boy about 14 years old: it was 12 at night. His window flung open. He went to shut it. He shut the window and dived into his bed. *Slam.* His window had flung open again, Jerry was confused and scared so he decided to lock the window. He could hear the cupboard shaking. 'Mum, Dad?' shouted Jerry! As he shouted for his parents, *bang,* the cupboard doors flew open and a figure in a hood jumped out with a knife. He tried to stab Jerry. His dad tackled him to the ground and phoned the police.

HARVEY WOODHAM (11)
Long Stratton High School, Norwich

I SAW A GHOST

The bird said to the mouse, 'I saw a ghost!'
The mouse replied, 'Yeah right!'
The bird said, 'I did, on the pier.'
The mouse replied, 'Show me tonight, on the pier, 7pm, it'll be dark by then!'

CERYS EMILY STYLES (11)
Long Stratton High School, Norwich

THE THING

In the gloom of the night a man was walking his dog. He let go of the lead, the dog ran. The man heard a whine then silence. He called for it and continued walking. Suddenly something grabbed him, the last thing he saw was white eyes, blood dripping mouth and the snarl. The monster crawled around looking for his next victim and meal. The thing crawled around, ate six cats, twelve dogs and don't forget the sixteen men, but it was not alone. I saw it. I experienced it. I lived it, it was me!

RUBY ANNE WOODHAM (11)
Long Stratton High School, Norwich

THE SAID TO BE HAUNTED HOUSE

We went in! It was dark with only one light. We went towards it. It got smaller! I stopped. My sister stopped. We had seen something bad. Very bad! It was our dead dad! He'd been eaten! The light went out. We shook with fear. A different light came on. In the corner, coming closer, was something horrible. A little girl. Alive? She put her head down, then back up again. Now she had no face! She disappeared! Another light came on. Under the spotlight was a jack-in-the-box, music playing. I had to get out. Now!

CODY GRAY (12)
Long Stratton High School, Norwich

THE RED EYES

'The forest is dark isn't it, boy?' I looked, he was gone. I called for
Sam, no dog came, I flashed my torch about. There was a rustle.
I turned just to glimpse a sight of red eyes disappearing into the
bushes, a shiver went up my spine. I ran not looking behind me,
I tripped into a ditch, damn, I twisted my ankle. I struggled under
some leaves. I felt something, it was my dog, lifeless. I held my
breath as I heard the crunching of leaves, then the black monster
disappeared. I laid there terrified, scared to breathe.

THOMAS JAMES ARMES (12)
Long Stratton High School, Norwich

NEVER PLAY ON STONES

The most painful day of my life! I thought it was just going to be a
normal day. It really wasn't. I blame my sister. Although, it was both
of us. My knee split open from one tiny stone. Before I knew it I was
sitting in the medical room in lots of pain so here's what happened.
My sister and I were playing on some slippery stones. She was
pulling me up and down. That's when it happened, she dropped me.
Even now there's a stone in my knee. Never ever play on slippery,
sharp stones after rain.

AMELIA CREASEY (11)
Long Stratton High School, Norwich

UNTITLED

The clock struck 12. Strong gusts of wind whistled in the trees. Light shone through the curtains. I crept over to the window. A black van was on the driveway. A shiver ran down my spine. I clambered into bed. 'Argh!' There was a high-pitched scream followed by an eerie silence. 'Katy, come pick me up now!' I texted. There was a knock on the door and I breathed a sigh of relief, but the door unlocked itself and all I could hear was the sound of my heart pounding. I felt a cold hand on my shoulder. 'Katy?'

AMY HUNT (12)
Long Stratton High School, Norwich

UNDER THE BED

Lilly always complained about strange noises under her bed!
One night they were really loud so she called her mother to check under the bed. Her mother slowly put her head under the bed to check what was happening. A knife came out and stabbed her in the lower chest! Lilly stood screaming and shrieking as her beloved mother lay dead and bleeding on her bedroom floor! Slowly a clown came out from under the bed! Blood dripped from the sides of his mouth. He took her back under the bed… Lilly was missing, never to come back home!

FREYA LOUISE SUMMERS (11)
Long Stratton High School, Norwich

Godzila Cow

Once there was a lost city called Cowlington. It was a peaceful city until a gigantic cow (later named Godzilla Cow) stormed through the barriers of it.

Suddenly, the police came flying out trying to shoot Godzilla Cow but he stamped on them. He trotted past the death scene killing innocent adults and children and his minions stabbed them with knives.

But at night Godzilla Cow turned into a clown that kept jumping into the sky and crashing down on houses shattering them into pieces and killing any people that were lurking scared of what would happen to them.

ELOISE ANNE WATKINS (12)
Long Stratton High School, Norwich

Alone

Alone I was. Standing on the bridge of the castle. The rusted chains holding me up. I could hear nothing except for creaking. It was pitch-black. My size 10 foot squelched as it made contact with the wood. There the castle towered above me. I opened the door. *Creak.* I walked, scared into the castle. 'Hello!' I carried on walking. Where would the prince be? I asked myself. I stepped. *Creak.* I turned quickly, there was a bear eyeing me. An eye of its fell out and a worm came out. The bear said, 'Hi, and very soon, 'Goodbye.'

BEN WAY (11)
Long Stratton High School, Norwich

Ding-Dong!

We were only exploring. The rusty door which belonged to the abandoned church was open so we ran in, not hesitating, up the creaky stairs to the top. The big bell that hadn't rang for years was just hanging there. We heard footsteps coming up the stairs. Someone entered the room. We hid behind the other side of the bell. Jack panicked, he ran and bumped into a figure. The man fell over the bars onto the bell and the ropes wrapped around him. *Ding-Dong!* That's all we can hear now ringing in our head. Never-ending.

LILY ALLUM (12)
Long Stratton High School, Norwich

Is This The End?

There was a silent smash inside of a haunted house with over-grown grass and trees growing really high with windows smashed. A 16-year-old girl called Eve heard the smash and shouted her nan. 'Nan, was that you?' There was no reply. She ran into the room where her nan was meant to be but then she remembered her nan was not alive anymore. Eve decided she would go and do some gardening. She saw her nan's gravestone. She was digging up the mud to plant some seeds and saw her nan's special pink bracelet and a hand.

CHLOE JOY-ANN HEWETT (12)
Long Stratton High School, Norwich

THE HORRIBLE HAUNTED HOUSE

As the sky darkened I walked up to the abandoned house. Nobody ever went in; nobody ever came out. As I walked further along the long, treacherous path, I felt more like the bare sky-high trees were staring at me and gleaming! When I reached the house I realised that the windows were smashed, but nevertheless I pushed the rusty handle down and went in! I looked around and I couldn't see anything, no furniture or even any evidence of people. But I could hear people, someone was calling me from the top of the stairs. 'Jake!'

HANNAH STARMAN (11)
Long Stratton High School, Norwich

UNTITLED

The boy was walking through the forest but then a voice said, 'Come to the biggest tree.' It was a long walk to the biggest tree, it took about ten minutes to get there. He stopped for something to eat first. The voice said, 'Hurry up before the time's up!' But the boy opened a bag of crisps before he set off to the biggest tree, but then a voice said, 'Five minutes left.'
He ran there. Luckily he got there in time. When he got there... 'Argh!'

MAX CHATTEN (11)
Long Stratton High School, Norwich

ABANDONED BUILDING

I looked behind me. I saw an empty building. I stepped inside. It looked like an old corridor. I entered the room. Suddenly, I heard a baby giggle so I turned around and on the wall were handprints of blood. It sent a shiver down my spine. I touched the prints. They were fresh behind me. I heard footsteps. I looked back at the prints, there were more. I could just make out two words: 'The End'. Everything suddenly went pitch-black. I couldn't see anything. Then a cold hand grabbed my shoulder and they didn't want to let go.

LUCY SELFE (12)
Long Stratton High School, Norwich

THE MAN AT THE END OF THE CORRIDOR

Hi, I'm Aston. I'm 14 and my friend and I are going to break into school. 'Hi Luke, are you ready?' Aston asked.
'Yeah,' Luke replied. When they got to school they went through their teachers' files to see their secrets. Then out of nowhere we heard a sound from the corridor. When Luke and I looked out of the room there was a weird figure chasing us. Then Luke and I all of a sudden fainted.
When I woke up I wasn't in school, I was in the hospital, with a stranger!

JAMIE WILKS (11)
Long Stratton High School, Norwich

THE END

'He knew there would be certain death if he touched the chest...'
I stood, transfixed, annoyed - did the visitors time have to be up?
We left the room and began the journey home, then I saw the nurse
running towards us. 'You have to come quickly!' Leading us to
Granny, my eyes instantly locked onto a monitor with a straight line
across the screen. I ran.
Granny's voice echoed, *'Death would come if he touched it...'* I
screamed. *'He lifted the lid...'* I closed my eyes and took a blow from a
wall. The nurse found me and nodded.

LILY RICHARDS (12)
Long Stratton High School, Norwich

THE FOREST TRIP

The thick mud squelched underneath my feet. The wind was blowing
and the trees squeaked. It was getting dark and I was lost. The mist
was thick and I was lost. I couldn't see the end of the path. Then I
heard a snap. My heart pounded. I was going to explode with fear.
I picked up the pace, my walk broke into a sprint. Something was
chasing me. Then I slipped. I quickly scrambled up. A cold hand
caught my leg. I got pulled back. I knew then that I was already
dead.

ALEX BIRD
Long Stratton High School, Norwich

UNTITLED

The windy clifftops in Scotland were deserted, but around the clifftops a boy was standing to the left. He was the bully. Five minutes later I was creeping up behind him, the sound of my footsteps broke the silence.
The next morning police asked me, 'What happened?'
I replied, 'He took the stone elevator.' I walked up to the edge of the cliff. I looked down the cliff and there, in the distance, was the body splatted on one of the stones below.

DYLAN SMITH (12)
Long Stratton High School, Norwich

MONSTERS ARE REAL

Jodie was asleep. Dreaming lovely dreams. Not thinking about the tragic news she'd been given. Jodie was born with an invisible friend that's under her control. Her friend told her about the monsters but… she wasn't told what time they would attack. As Jodie slept she didn't realise a shadow that was lurking over her head. Suddenly… 'Argh!' Jodie screamed in fear. Her parents ran into the room and found her covered in cuts and shivering on the floor saying, 'Monsters are real!' repeatedly.

SARAH DODMAN (11)
Long Stratton High School, Norwich